D0066015

FLOWERS OF DARKNESS

FLOWERS OF DARKNESS

TATIANA DE ROSNAY

ST. MARTIN'S PRESS
NEW YORK

First published in the United States by St. Martin's Press, an imprint of St. Martin's Publishing Group

FLOWERS OF DARKNESS. Copyright © 2021 by Tatiana de Rosnay. All rights reserved. Printed in the United States of America. For information, address St. Martin's Publishing Group, 120 Broadway, New York, NY 10271.

www.stmartins.com

The Library of Congress Cataloging-in-Publication Data is available upon request.

ISBN 978-1-250-27255-3 (hardcover)
ISBN 978-1-250-27290-4 (ebook)

Our books may be purchased in bulk for promotional, educational, or business use. Please contact your local bookseller or the Macmillan Corporate and Premium Sales Department at 1-800-221-7945, extension 5442, or by email at MacmillanSpecialMarkets@macmillan.com.

Originally published in France by Éditions Robert Laffont

First Edition: 2020
First U.S. Edition: 2021

10 9 8 7 6 5 4 3 2 1

To my father,
who taught me how to look at the future

Not only our memories, but the things we have forgotten are "housed." Our subconscious is "housed." Our soul is an abode.

—*The Poetics of Space,* Gaston Bachelard

CONTENTS

FLOWERS OF DARKNESS

1

ঙ্গ্চ

KEY

So I am doing what seems the best thing to do.
VIRGINIA WOOLF, March 28, 1941

This can obviously be held accountable to a nervous breakdown.
ROMAIN GARY, December 2, 1980

S HE VISITED TWENTY APARTMENTS before finding the right one. Nobody could imagine what an ordeal it had been, especially for a writer obsessed with houses, with what walls remembered. The building had been completed last year. It wasn't far from the Tower, or what was left of the Tower. After the attack, the neighborhood had suffered. For years, the place remained a dusty and wrecked no-man's-land ignored by all. Little by little, the vicinity was able to rise from its ashes. Architects had thought out harmonious neoclassical structures, as well as a vast green garden including the memorial and the space where the identical Tower was yet to be rebuilt. With the passing of time, this part of town had been able to recover its serenity. Tourists came flocking back.

Mrs. Dalloway's soft voice was heard.

"Clarissa, you have incoming emails. One is from Mia White, not in your contact list, and one is from your father. Do you wish to read them now?"

Her father! She checked her watch. One A.M. in Paris, midnight in London, and the old chap was still awake. Getting on for ninety-eight and full of beans.

"I'll read them later, Mrs. Dalloway. Please turn the computer off. And the lights in the living room."

In the beginning, she had felt guilty, bossing Mrs. Dalloway around. But she had gotten used to it. It was quite pleasurable, in fact. Mrs. Dalloway never appeared. She was merely a voice. But Clarissa knew Mrs. Dalloway had eyes and ears in every room. Clarissa often wondered what she would have looked like, had she existed. It was believed Virginia Woolf modeled Mrs. Dalloway's character after a woman named Kitty Maxse, a frivolous party giver who had been a close friend, and who had met a tragic end, tumbling over her own banisters. Clarissa had looked up Kitty Maxse, and discovered photographs of a perfectly groomed lady with an hourglass figure and a dainty parasol.

She stood in the dark living room, facing the window, clasping the cat close to her. The computer no longer glowed into the deepening darkness. Would she ever get used to this flat? It wasn't so much the smell of new paint. There was something else. She couldn't quite place it. She loved the view, though. High up above the ground level, away from the action, she felt safe, tucked into her own private shelter. Was she really safe? she wondered as the cat purred against her and the black night seemed to hem her in. Safe from what, safe from whom? Living alone was proving to be more difficult than she'd thought. She wondered what François was doing now. He was still in their old apartment. She imagined him in their living room, binge-watching a TV show, feet up on the table. What was the point of thinking of François? No point at all.

Clarissa's shortsighted eyes gazed down to the street, far below, where tipsy vacationers staggered, their laughter wafting up to her in a muffled roar. This new area of the city was never empty. Hordes of tourists materialized ceaselessly on sidewalks, in a dusty synchronicity that befuddled her. She had learned to avoid certain boulevards, where swarms of sightseers stood, vacuously, brandishing cell phones at what remained of the Tower, and the construction site of the new one. She had to wade through their compact mass, sometimes even had to elbow through them in order to get past.

Watching the building across the street and all those beings behind each window would never tire her. Within the past weeks, since she'd been living here, she'd learned to pick out each occupant's routine. She already knew who was sleepless, like she was, who worked late in front of a screen, who enjoyed a snack in the middle of the night. She couldn't be seen; she was too high up, tucked away behind the stone cornices. Sometimes, she used her field glasses. She never felt guilty, although she would hate it if anyone spied on her that way. She always checked to see if someone was looking back at her. And even if no one was, why did she still feel an eye upon her?

Other people's lives unfolded in front of her, enticing alveoli forming a giant hive in which she could forage at her will, fueling her imagination boundlessly. Each opening was like a Hopper painting, lush with detail. The second-floor woman did her yoga every morning on a mat she rolled out with care. The third-floor family never stopped bickering. The slamming of those doors! The person on the sixth spent hours in the bathroom (yes, she could see through panes that weren't opaque enough). The lady of her age on the fifth floor daydreamed on her sofa. She didn't know their names, but she knew nearly everything about their daily existence. And it fascinated her.

When she started to look for her new abode, she hadn't realized to what extent she was going to trespass into unknown people's intimacy. Each room told a story by the disposition of its furniture, objects, through odors, scents, and colors. She had only to walk into a living room to extricate a prescient vision of the person who lived there. She could picture the inhabitant's life entirely in one dizzying and addictive flash. She saw it all, as if she had been provided with special internal sensors.

She'd never forget the duplex flat situated on boulevard Saint-Germain, near Odéon. The description fit her needs perfectly. She liked the neighborhood, and already visualized herself trotting up the polished stairs daily. But once she was inside, the ceiling was so low, she practically had to hunch her back. The real estate agent had asked, jokingly, how tall she was. What an idiot! She was able to tell right away the owner worked in publishing, because of all the manuscripts piled up on the black lacquered desk. Some editors still revised texts on paper, but they were exceedingly rare. The bookshelves were full of hardcovers and paperbacks, a vision of joy for a writer. She tilted her head to read the titles. Yes, there were two of hers there, *Topography of Intimacy* and *The Sleep Thief.* It hadn't been the first time she'd seen her own books while visiting a flat, but it invariably brought her pleasure.

The duplex was lovely, but miniature. She couldn't stand properly in any of the rooms; her body ate up all the space, like Alice in Wonderland becoming larger than the house. It was a shame, because the premises were sunny, quiet, giving on to a pretty interior courtyard. She hadn't been able to stop herself from looking at the beauty products in the bathroom, perfume and makeup, and when the agent had opened the wardrobe, she had taken in the clothes and high-heeled pumps. Swiftly, the portrait of a woman had arisen: small, dainty, spick-and-span, young still, but alone. No love in her life. Something dry and barren permeated the place, shadowed the walls, upholstered the air. In the glossy brown bedchamber, the mattress had the funereal aspect of a tombstone, where all she could perceive was a recumbent effigy, petrified by a century-long torpor. No one ever had orgasms within these walls, either alone or in company. A profound gloom oozed from the immaculate and silent rooms. She had fled.

She began to see a flat a day. One time, she had felt sure she'd found the right home, at last. A cheerful fifth-floor flat with a balcony, near the Madeleine. It was sunny, one of her priorities. It had recently been renovated and the décor suited her. The owner was moving back to Switzerland. Since the attacks, his wife didn't wish to go on living in the city. Clarissa had just been about to sign the lease, when she noticed, to her dismay, the existence of a rugby pub on the ground floor. She had always come in the morning, and hadn't paid attention, as the bar was closed. She had returned later in the evening just to get a feel of the area at nighttime and had made the discovery. The pub opened every evening and operated until two o'clock in the morning. Jordan, her daughter, had made fun of her. So what? She could use earplugs, couldn't she? But Clarissa hated those. She decided to test the noise level by spending the night in a small hotel across from the pub.

"We have nice quiet rooms in the back," said the receptionist when she checked in.

"No, no", she replied, "I want to be in front of the pub."

He had stared at her.

"You won't get much sleep. Even if there's no game on, you'll still get a lot of noise. And in the summertime, I can't even begin to tell you what it's like. The neighbors complain all the time."

She had thanked him and held out her hand for the card. He was right. Clients chatting on the sidewalk, pint in hand, had awakened her steadily until two in the morning. Every time the pub doors opened, loud music could be heard, very clearly, in spite of the double glazing. She called the agency the next morning and said she wouldn't be taking the flat.

Everything she ended up seeing failed to suit her. She began to lose hope. François had tried to hold her back. Didn't she want to stay? She hadn't wanted to hear a single word. Had he gone crazy? After everything he'd done? Did he really think she was going to shut up and stick around? Act like nothing had happened? When she had become desperate, and was even contemplating moving to London, into the dismal basement flat rented out to students in her father's house in Hackney, she met Guillaume at the inaugural cocktail party for a bookstore-café in Montparnasse. She hadn't planned to stay long, but the owner, Nathalie, was a fervent supporter of her work. The opening of a shop that sold books was such a rare event that she decided to go, and also out of friendship for Nathalie.

She was introduced to a trim young man called Guillaume, a friend of Nathalie's. He swiftly explained he had nothing to do with publishing, that calamitous business; he was into real estate. He offered her a glass of champagne, which she accepted. After the attack, the major part of the seventh arrondissement had to be rethought and rebuilt: everything situated between the Tower and the École Militaire, and between avenue de la Bourdonnais and boulevard de Grenelle. His firm had been chosen in order to reconstruct the area along the old track of avenue Charles-Floquet. Like most Parisians, Clarissa was aware that the streets and avenues that had been destroyed had been rebuilt differently, with new names. There had been an emphasis on foliage and vegetation. A peacefulness much needed by all, Guillaume had pointed out.

Clarissa had never envisaged that recent neighborhood. It was probably expensive, she said to herself, out of her league. Guillaume proudly described the accommodation he'd created with his team, showing her photos on his mobile device. She admitted it was magnificent. Verdant, contemporary, striking. He chimed his number and emailed it to her phone. All she had to do, if ever she wanted more information, was to send him a text.

"Are there any flats available?" she asked tentatively.

"That's complicated," he said. "Yes, technically, there are, but they're reserved for artists. There's a quota we need to keep to."

She asked what he meant by "artists." He shrugged, scratched his head. He meant painters, musicians, poets, singers, sculptors. There was a special residence just for them. But no one publicized it; otherwise, they'd be swamped. In order to get in, there were interviews, presentations, in front of a committee. Quite a thing. Serious stuff! Not many people made it.

"What about writers? Haven't you forgotten them?"

She was right; he had forgotten writers. They were indeed artists, just as much as the others.

"Can you tell me how I can sign up?"

Obviously, he had no idea who she was, what she did. She didn't mind; after all, her latest success had been published a while ago. She pulled him by the sleeve, all the way to the bookshelf labeled "K," slid out *Topography of Intimacy,* and handed it to him under Nathalie's curious gaze as she chatted a little farther away. He leafed through it, and said he was sorry he did not know more about her and her work. He never read books. He didn't have time to read. Politely, he asked her what it was about.

"It's about writers and the link between their work, their homes, their intimacy, and their suicides, particularly Virginia Woolf and Romain Gary. It's a novel, not an essay."

He was taken aback, staring down at the cover, where Gary's blue eyes made an interesting contrast with Woolf's dark ones.

"Ah, yes" was all he could bring himself to say. He looked at her for the first time, and Clarissa knew what he was thinking, that she must have been good-looking once, and that, curiously, she still was.

He suggested she contact a woman named Clémence Dutilleul, via a specific website, of which he gave her the address. She was the person who dealt with admissions concerning the artists' residence. Clarissa had to hurry. There were very few vacancies. When she returned to the studio she rented weekly in order not to endure her husband's presence, she went online to the website. She was certain she didn't stand a chance, but why not register? That same night, she filled out a detailed questionnaire and sent it through a link to Clémence Dutilleul. She was most surprised to get an answer the next morning, and a proposal for a meeting scheduled the day after.

"Do you really want to live where all those people were killed?" Jordan's voice was ironic. "Especially you, obsessed with places? You've written about that over and over again. Won't you be getting into trouble? You'll never be able to sleep!"

Clarissa tried to defend herself by stating that living in a city like Paris meant she walked over bloody tragedy every day, in every step she took. The new buildings attracted her because they had no past.

Clarissa went into the kitchen; the lights turned on as she glided by. Light switches had disappeared years ago, and she rather liked it. She had been told, when she moved in last month, that she could name the apartment's virtual assistant with a term of her own choosing.

"Mrs. Dalloway, turn on the kettle."

Mrs. Dalloway complied. Clarissa left most household matters to her. The heating, air conditioner, alarm, shutters, lighting scheme, automatic cleaning system, and all sorts of other tasks were under Mrs. Dalloway's expert supervision. Clarissa was still getting used to it. She had hesitated between "Mrs. Danvers" and "Mrs. Dalloway" at first, before her unconditional veneration for

Virginia Woolf had prevailed. And there was something rather frightening about Mrs. Danvers in Daphne du Maurier's *Rebecca*. Clarissa was alone now, in this flat, without her husband of many years. The tall, gaunt black figure of the devoted housekeeper, Manderley's disquieting sentinel, was not a reassuring one. She was still trying to find her marks in this brand-new dwelling. Clarissa Dalloway seemed a far more comforting character, and she had inspired half of her pen name, after all.

She prepared herbal tea, added a dollop of honey. It was artificial, of course, and tasted sugary and creamy. The real stuff was impossible to find. She had obtained a tiny treasured amount last year, through a clandestine connection, but at what price! Honey was now more expensive than caviar. So were flowers. Sometimes she pined for the smell of real roses, like the ones that had grown in her mother's garden long ago. Fake roses were rather cleverly manufactured; they even boasted drops of false dew, twinkling like diamonds in their crimson hearts. The petals felt velvety at first, but soon a rubbery consistence took over. After a while, their pungent perfume revealed a nasty chemical whiff she could no longer stand.

As she sipped the herbal tea and looked out to the rooftops across from her, she thought, not for the first time, that perhaps she had chosen this apartment too hastily in the wake of her sudden decision to leave François. Perhaps she should have given the move more thought. Was this the right place for her? The cat was her daughter's idea. Jordan had told her cats were the perfect pets for writers. For solitary writers? Clarissa had asked. But just how solitary had she really wanted to be? The living room stretched out in front of her, its elegant minimalism still an enigma to her unaccustomed eye. It looked beautiful, but empty.

Once she had decided to leave her husband, it had been a mad rush. She had believed, and how wrong she had been, that a new lodging was going to be easy to find. She wasn't set on anything big, or fancy; she simply needed a room to work in. A room of one's own, as her dear Virginia Woolf said. A living room and one bedroom, so that Adriana, nicknamed "Andy," her granddaughter, could still come and spend the night. She wasn't fussy either about the area she wanted to live in, as long as shopping was easy and public transport available. Nobody drove cars in the city. She had even forgotten how to drive. Another thing François and Jordan had done for her, on holiday. Now it was going to be Jordan's job.

The cat rubbed against her shins. She stooped to pick him up, catching him clumsily, as she wasn't used to handling him yet. Her daughter had shown her how, but it hadn't seemed easy. The cat's name was Chablis. He was a three-year-old Chartreux with a mild nature. He'd belonged to one of Jordan's friends, a woman who had moved to the States. It had been tough in the beginning. Chablis had stayed in his corner, never responding to her calls, and only deigned to nibble at his nuggets when she wasn't there. She thought maybe he was sad and missed his mistress. Then one day, he came to sit on her lap in a very dignified manner, as still as a gray sphinx. She had hardly dared pet him.

Chablis, like her, was finding it tricky to adapt to the luminous and modern space, built with glass and honey-hued wood and stone. However, a part of her liked the austerity, the sleek surfaces, the light. She and the cat would have to make this territory their own, and that would take time. Patience was needed. She had left behind so much stuff when she moved in. She hadn't wanted anything emotionally stamped with François. As if he had died. But the worst thing was, he had not died. He was, in fact, doing very well—insolently well. It was their marriage that had passed away. It was their marriage she had laid to rest.

Clarissa put Chablis into the basket placed in a corner of her room. It was useless, because in the middle of the night, the cat landed gently on her bed and burrowed against her back. When he had started to knead her shoulder with his front paws, as if she were a slab of tasty dough, she was startled. Jordan had explained that all cats did that; it was instinctive. She had gotten used to it. In fact, it comforted her.

After a quick shower, Clarissa lay down on her bed in the semi-darkness. A new mattress. François had not slept on it. He had not been here, either. She hadn't invited him. Would she? It was still too early. She hadn't taken it all in. Several times, Jordan had asked what was it that her stepfather was guilty of, to make her mother pack up and leave on the spot. She could have told her. Jordan was forty-four. No longer a kid. She had a teenage daughter. But she hadn't had the courage. Jordan had insisted. What had he done? Had he screwed around? Was he in love? Clarissa thought of the purple room, the blond curls. She could tell her daughter everything. She knew exactly which words to use. She imagined Jordan's face. She had let the words rise to her lips, like a bitter bile, and had repressed them.

Forget François. But it wasn't easy to scrap a man she'd spent so many years with. When night came, she asked Mrs. Dalloway to project images and videos on the ceiling of her room: concerts by musicians she loved, movies, biopics, artistic creations. She let sounds and lights drift her away, often falling asleep. She couldn't draw a frontier between her peculiar, sparkling dreams and Mrs. Dalloway's displays. Sometimes, she let Mrs. Dalloway choose sequences picked according to what she had already seen. She didn't see the night float by. Everything converged into a single tawdry cotillion she endured, as if she had been drugged. When she woke up, the cat snuggled against her; she found it hard to get out of bed, and her mouth was dry. Early mornings had seemed harsh ever since she'd moved here. Her entire body felt sore. She put it down to the collapse of her marriage, and the move. Would she ever get used to both?

"Mrs. Dalloway, show me my emails."

The messages appeared on the ceiling.

Dear Clarissa Katsef,

I know you get dozens of emails like these, but I thought I'd give it a go. My name is Mia White. I'm nineteen. I'm a student at UEA, in Norwich. I'm in my second year. I'm studying French and English literature. I'm also enrolled in a creative writing course.

(If you've read this far, then I pray you might continue?)

I'm interested in how places influence writers. How their work is shaped by where they live, where they write. This, of course, is at the core of your own work, and in particular, *Topography of Intimacy,* which I read with great pleasure.

(This is not a gooey fan letter, don't worry. I'm not that type of reader.)

I will be in Paris for the next six months, for my year abroad. I'm sure you're very busy and you don't have much time, but I'd like to meet you. I'm also bilingual, like you, and I grew up learning two languages, like you. My mum is French and my dad is English. Like you.

I don't know if you make time to meet your readers. Perhaps you don't.

Thank you for reading this.

Sincerely,
Mia White

Clarissa took off her glasses, rubbed her eyes. No, she didn't usually meet readers, apart from book signings and lectures. She used to, ten or fifteen years ago. Not anymore. Mia White. It was interesting, refreshing, getting an email from a nineteen-year-old. Didn't that mean that a tiny minority still read books? And that they read her books? Wasn't that short of miraculous?

Hardly anyone read books anymore. She'd noticed that a while ago. People were glued to their phones, to their devices. Bookstores shut down, one after the other. Her biggest success, *Topography of Intimacy,* had been hacked so many times, it hardly brought in any royalties. It could be found online and downloaded in a single click, in any language. At first, Clarissa had put up a fuss, tried to warn her publisher, but she soon realized publishers were not doing much against piracy. They had other anxieties. They had to face that other, even more worrying problem she watched thrive month after month like a sly tumor: the loss of interest in reading. Yes, it seemed no one yearned for books anymore. No one bought them. This had been going on for quite a while. The phenomenal space social media gobbled up in everyone's life was no doubt a reason for this disaffection. The frenetic succession of attacks strung one after the other like bloody pearls on a steadfast necklace of violence was another. Mobile phone snug in her palm, she, too, had found herself hypnotized by atrocious images scalding her with the abomination of sheer detail. She understood that to those addicted to such displays of barbarity, those constantly seeking more sensationalism like a junkie hankering for a fix, novels could appear savorless. It took time to read a book. As it took time to write one. And it appeared no one had the time to read or write anymore.

"Would you like to answer Mia White?" asked Mrs. Dalloway.

"No. Later. Show me the other emails."

She put her glasses back on. Her father's email showed up now on the ceiling. She knew he dictated them. His arthritis prevented him from using a keyboard. He didn't do too badly. His punctuation was poor, but he made himself clear. She corresponded with him by email. He didn't hear well enough anymore to speak to her by phone or video. Probably something wrong with his hearing chip. She hadn't told him yet about François.

My darling C . . . [he still used her real name, which she hated],
     I'm ok and you. Your brother's been looking after me but the
damn boy's got better things to do. I'm so bored you know. Most
of my friends are dead and those who are still here are so fucking

boring you can't imagine. I know you haven't spoken to your brother since that shitty inheritance business. My sister was a selfish pain in the ass. Really how could she possibly leave all her money to Arthur's daughters and nothing to Jordan. I still can't get over it. I know you don't want to discuss this and that it hurts you but it hurts me too. Arthur has been a letdown to you his only sister but to me his father as well. He could have done something about the will. Give an amount to Jordan. What the fuck. He did nothing. I know Jordan doesn't speak to her cousins. What sluts. They don't have an ounce of your daughter's class and brains. Serena's inheritance totally screwed up this family. Thank God your mum is no longer here to see this mess. Darling please give me some news. I'm your old dad and even if I can't make heads or tails of the intellectual stuff you write I'm so proud of you. You know you haven't written to me in two weeks. Why and what the hell is going on. I asked Andy how you were. She always answers me not like her granny. She told me you had moved. What is going on. Where are you living now. I loved your flat near the Luxembourg gardens so why did you leave. Did François decide this. Or you. I'm sad I don't get it. Come on tell me. Everything. Every email from you is like a little gift. It lights up my day. I miss you sweetheart. Come and see your old dad one of these days. I'm too old to come to Paris. I'm counting on you. Your old dad who loves you.

She couldn't help smiling. Her father wrote the way he spoke. She could almost see him in his ground-floor lair, surrounded by his hunting trophies, his golf clubs, and his collection. He collected ancient representations of hands, made of clay, porcelain, marble, plaster, wood, or wax. She had often brought some back for him, harvested during her book tours. So Adriana had let the cat out of the bag. Perhaps a good thing. She'd have to think carefully about what to tell her father. He wasn't particularly fond of

François, which hadn't been the case with her first husband, Toby, Jordan's father.

"Do you wish to answer your father's email?" asked Mrs. Dalloway.

"Not now," she said. And then she added, "Thank you."

"You're welcome, Clarissa."

There was even a hint of a smile in Mrs. Dalloway's voice. Like any virtual assistant, Mrs. Dalloway knew everything. She could answer any question, come up with the right answer each time. But Clarissa knew Mrs. Dalloway had also been programmed with specific data concerning herself. What, precisely? She hadn't been able to find out. When she had met Clémence Dutilleul, she had undergone a surprising interview. The C.A.S.A. headquarters were also situated within the new neighborhoods that had sprung from the cinders of the attack. A tall glass-and-steel building with a rooftop garden. Clémence's office gave on to that top floor. It was a vast and airy room with a view. The pale walls were paneled with mirrors. From here, Clarissa could see how the new white zone contrasted with the old Haussmannian gray-slated arteries, but it was a welcome, hopeful sight, she felt.

Clémence was a small, thin woman in her early forties. She wore a black suit, which had a 1940s aspect to it, giving her a severe elegance Clarissa rather liked. She had no idea what to expect. There was no information about the interviews on the website, and she hadn't found anything online. The C.A.S.A. artists' residence remained shrouded in mystery. A short man in his fifties came to join them, and she didn't catch his name. The interviews took place around a white oval table. A young man came to offer them tea and coffee. Clarissa had decided not to dress up for this. Most of her clothes were still in the flat she shared with François. She wanted to be seen exactly as she was. What was the point of pretending to be someone else? She wore a green shirt, white jeans, and sneakers. Her red hair was braided. She was convinced she would never get in anyhow. She was too old, not famous enough, she didn't sell enough books, she wasn't trendy. There were probably hundreds of younger, brighter candidates on their list. She hoped this wouldn't be too humiliating.

They had no files in front of them. Not even a device, a pen, or a piece of paper. They asked her if she minded being filmed. Yet she couldn't see a camera anywhere. She said, no problem. She wondered where the camera was hidden. The man in his fifties had a pleasant face. It was his eyes that bothered her, how they took her in. Two black shiny marbles that never left her.

Clémence sipped her coffee, and beamed. The silence lasted, and it didn't bother Clarissa. She wasn't afraid of silence. If they were expecting her to talk, to fill in the blanks, then they were wrong. She wasn't going to come across as eager, or even desperate. She had nothing to lose. So she smiled back. There was probably an invisible team, tucked away in the building, or perhaps behind one of those mirrors, watching her every move, dissecting whatever she did.

"Thank you very much for coming in today," said Clémence Dutilleul at last.

The man with the shiny black eyes spoke up.

"This has nothing to do with a formal interview. The conversation we'll be having is meant to be a relaxed, cordial one. Not an examination. We want to hear you talk about yourself, about your work. Our artists' residence is a real estate elaboration that holds great promise. We crafted it so that people like you, artists, can live and work there serenely. We need to get to know you a little better. We're not interested in what's already been said or written about you. However, what does interest us is your own approach to your artistic output and the implementation of your body of work. We want to know more about your career history, your development. You can take all the time you wish, or, on the contrary, be succinct. It doesn't matter. What does matter is the quality of your project and your artistic endeavor. I hope I've been clear, now. Over to you."

Two grins, slightly inflexible, and two pairs of inquisitive eyes. A fit of giggles nearly swept over her for a quick moment. Where should she begin? She hated talking about herself, and always had. She hadn't prepared anything, no speech, no presentation. She couldn't stand authors who took themselves seriously, who delighted in their own rhetoric. She couldn't figure out what criteria these people's selection process depended on. *However, what does interest us is your own approach to your own artistic output and the implementation of your body of work.* What the fuck, as her dad would say. She made up her mind fast. She was going to be to the point. Her application was never going to be chosen anyway. In ten minutes, she'd be out of here.

"I've just left my husband."

It just slipped out. She hadn't meant to bring up her personal life. Too bad. They were still staring at her attentively, nodding. She went on.

She explained she had never lived alone. She had to feel good within a home, not only in order to live there but to write there, as well. She was looking for an apartment that could be a sort of shelter. A haven that would keep her safe, that would protect her. Fittingly, her work explored houses and homes, what they conveyed. She had come to writing late in life. She was already over fifty by the time her first novel was published. The path to writing had opened up as she had pieced together the link between writers and places. She hadn't planned on writing a book at all. The novel foisted itself upon her after a personal tragedy and her discovery of hypnosis. It had been published, almost by chance, after a series of encounters, and it had done well. There was something else she wanted to tell them. In her opinion, artists don't need to explain their work. If people didn't get the gist of it or became sidelined, that was their problem. Why should an artist be heard? Creation spoke for itself. Occasionally, readers asked her to explain the endings of her books. It made her chuckle, weep at times, or even become downright furious. She wrote to make others think, not to give them answers.

She realized her voice was loud, ringing out within the huge room, and her hands were waving around. The video team was probably sniggering while they filmed. No doubt they had crossed her name off the list.

"Please go on," said the man with the glasses.

She replied that she didn't have much more to add. Oh, just one last point. She had been raised by a British father and a French mother; she was perfectly bilingual. She had two writing languages and had never been able to pick one over the other. So she had used both. This was a well-known fact about her. The difference was that today she had started to write in both languages at the same time. This was the first time, ever, that she had chosen to do this.

"That's most interesting," said Clémence slowly. "Could you please tell us more?"

They ogled her with the same yearning. What glistening, voracious eyes!

Could she trust them? They had such intense stares. She said that no, she couldn't tell them more. Aptly, she was planning to write about just that: what it meant to have a hybrid brain that wrote in two languages simultaneously. It was a new project and it was too early for her to talk about it. Her editor wasn't even aware of her project. It was difficult to describe an idea as it was thriving. But she knew how deeply the subject touched her, how personal it was, and she intended to get to the bottom of it. She had always found bilingualism and its mechanisms riveting. She wanted to take time to explore it, to take ownership of it.

"A fascinating topic," said the man.

Clarissa was expecting to leave. She was due to visit a two-room apartment this afternoon, near La Fourche Métro station. A neighborhood she barely knew.

"We will be back shortly," announced Clémence with a wide smile. "Please wait for us here."

She was left alone in the large room with its mirrored walls. What had they gone to do? To discuss her candidacy with their team? Did she have a chance? She appeared to have attracted their attention with the bilingual-writing business. Was she still being filmed? For a short moment, she sat motionless. Then she got up, walked across to the terrace. She didn't care if they were still watching her. The garden was beautiful, but artificial, with fake perfumes floating over the false hedge. Box trees had never recovered from the destructive Asian moth attacks years ago. They had been utterly defoliated and had not been able to regain their past splendor. She fingered lavender, sea oat grasses, bonsai, daylilies. She had to admit the plants felt almost real. She hadn't seen a genuine garden in such a long time. This one was almost like the real thing. Almost. There was something too perfect about it. Nature, she remembered, was messier. The silence was eerie. No more insects. Not the faintest hum or buzz. No more birds. No chirping, no twittering. From down below, very little noise, either. Parts of the new neighborhood were entirely pedestrian, served by self-driving electric cars. Occasionally, the quaint clip-clop of hooves could be heard. Police patrols had taken to riding horses since the attacks, and she loved the sound. It gave the city an old-fashioned feel she treasured.

She glanced northward, to Montmartre. François's secret studio was near there. What was he going to do about it? He probably continued going there. She forced herself not to think about him. She still felt devastated by the trauma she'd endured in that place. She must obtain a flat in the C.A.S.A. artists' residence. Otherwise, she was not going to make it. She was going to drift away. There was no way she could keep her chin up anymore. All her vulnerabilities became apparent, rising up to overwhelm the barricades she had patiently built up, year after year, since the baby's death, all that time ago. She felt desperate, weak. Never had she endured such intense loneliness. Whom could she confide in? What she had to say was unspeakable. She felt ashamed, too, and she resented her husband for inflicting that shame upon her. She hated him. She despised him. Her disappointment was colossal. She hadn't even been able to tell him that. She had nearly spat in his face. All she had been capable of doing was to pack in silence, hands trembling, while he wept. Not finding an apartment worried her. She was haunted by the prospect of a new home, just for her. A new place, with no past, no traces of anything. Her shelter. An intimate space. Her fortress. She thought of all the flats she'd seen. The idea of having to see more of them depressed her.

"Here we are!"

Clémence's voice made her jump. They were standing in front of her. In the bright daylight, she noticed the creases in their clothes, the fine dandruff on the man's shoulders. She was invited to come back inside. She was offered another cup of tea. She took it, intrigued by their leisureliness. They didn't seem in any hurry. What did they want? What were they expecting from her?

"We'd like to show you something," announced Clémence.

A screen materialized on one of the mirrors. Photos of a luminous apartment with a skylight appeared. The C.A.S.A. logo was clearly visible on the bottom left.

"This is our artist's studio," said the man. "Eighty square meters."

"Facing northwest and south. Full of light," added Clémence. "Top floor, the eighth."

Why were they showing her these photographs? A floor plan showed up now: a large main room, an open kitchen, a small study, a bedroom, and a bathroom. It all seemed low-key, tasteful, elegant.

"Preparation will be necessary; it will take half a day," said the man. "You'll have to come back. Nothing complicated, no need to worry. All you'll have to do is answer a series of questions. Security, maintenance, and a personal assistant for the apartment need to be set up. Then you'll also meet Dr. Dewinter, who's in charge of the artists of the residence. She runs the C.A.S.A. program."

Wild hope surged through her. Had they chosen her? Had she made it? Was she going to be able to get on with her life, away from François? These people were so odd. What sort of game were they playing?

"I haven't quite understood why you are mentioning the apartment."

"Mrs. Katsef, your candidacy has been accepted. We're delighted."

She wanted to dance around the table. But she held back. Her age, her experience. She gave them a charming smile. She said she was delighted, as well. Could she see the place? She was told she could, and no later than this evening. When could she have the keys? Move in?

Clémence Dutilleul beamed again.

"You can move in shortly. But you won't be needing keys, or a pass."

Clarissa looked at her, baffled.

"Your retina will be your key to enter the lobby on the ground level. And your right index finger will open up the door of your studio. Keys and badges are done. Things of the past. Welcome to C.A.S.A., Mrs. Katsef."

❦

NOTEBOOK

I'm not quite sure when it started. There had been warning signs, but I hadn't paid attention to them. I guess I hadn't wanted to see. I began to notice he was often late, or that I couldn't get hold of him during the day. Most of the times, his phone was switched off, and I began to find that strange.

We had been through this before. Moments of pain I did not want to go back to. That dreadful instant when the suspicion takes over. When you can think of nothing else.

We had been through what many couples go through. Those bitter, painful, intimate moments where infidelity rears its head. It happens. And it had already happened quite a bit to us. He had always said the other women were not important. I had always managed to forgive.

Why had I been so lenient? I wonder now. With years comes a new kind of power. The idea that you don't want anyone taking advantage of you anymore. The inner conviction that you have had enough.

It doesn't happen overnight. It builds up slowly, like a thick liquid taking ages to boil. It took a while, for me.

There had been a truce. And it had lasted for years. He had been ill for quite a stretch. I suppose any thought of an affair had not gone through his head, nor mine. We were too busy tending to him, making sure he would pull through. His medication exhausted him. He slept most of the time.

I helped him get better, stayed by his side, listened to him. I got on with my life, wrote my books, wrote my TV shows, saw my daughter, my granddaughter, my friends.

He regained his strength and the illness became a bad memory. He got back to work, spent time with his team, and traveled. Sometimes he left for a day or two.

I'm trying to think back to what made me understand something was going on. The exact minute when I came out of the fog. The second I knew he was seeing another woman.

He had been late. He usually was, so I hadn't paid attention. We were having dinner at the home of some friends, and he turned up with a bouquet of flowers, mumbling some excuse.

It wasn't till later, when we got home, while he was in the bathroom, that I noticed the hair on his jacket. Long and blond. I remember saying to myself that this was like a scene out of a bad movie. Terribly clichéd. And yet there it was, that long golden hair stretching out like a snake on the sleeve of his jacket.

I didn't say anything. Then I reached out for his jacket, put my nose against the collar. I picked it out immediately.

Another perfume lingering there.

I sometimes wonder. If I had noticed anything earlier, if I had done something, would that have changed the course of events?

I don't think so. Everything was leading up to that moment.

Me, standing in front of that door, holding the key in my hand.

The key to Blue Beard's secret room.

2

❧

LAKE

If anybody could have saved me, it would have been you.
Virginia Woolf, March 28, 1941

Devotees of broken hearts should apply elsewhere.
Romain Gary, December 2, 1980

T HE CAT HAD been acting strangely for the past week. Clarissa thought perhaps she should bring it up with Jordan. Chablis ate less and less, and seemed to mew for hours. But what truly alarmed her was when he jumped, startled, as if he had seen or heard someone—the oddest thing. And yet, there was no one. No one, apart from herself. Silence ruled, always. Maybe the cat wasn't used to it yet. Neither was she. There had been a perpetual racket in the flat she'd shared with François. Noisy neighbors, doors banging, people gabbing in the street below, under their windows. She had only ever lived in ground-floor or second-floor apartments before the C.A.S.A. residence. The early-morning glow dazzled her each day when she awoke. She didn't need to ask Mrs. Dalloway to turn on any more lights. It was like living in the sky, in the clouds.

She had never anticipated she'd feel this lonely. She missed

François. She missed him at unexpected moments. A blues tune on the radio. A whiff of Vétiver. The sweater he'd given her after a weekend in Ireland. Even if all the furniture was new, even if she'd painstakingly erased all traces of her past and all traces of François, her husband was still there. He materialized like a watermark interlaced into every nook of the apartment. She could even make out his sturdy, slightly stubby-legged outline, the one she had cherished for so long. There he was, sprawled on the sofa, poring over his device. There he was, under the shower, lathering up foam. There he was, asking Mrs. Dalloway for a cappuccino. François had never cared about being smaller than she was. He had no hang-ups about his height. On the contrary, he was proud to have her at his arm. Now that she'd left him, should she call her friends? She wondered what he had told those same friends about their breakup. He couldn't conceivably have given them the truth. He must have spun a story. But which one? And what would she, in turn, say to her friends? She imagined their dismayed faces. Their pity. No, she must keep it bottled up. François would do the same thing. He didn't have much choice.

No matter how hard she tried not to, she imagined him walking up the rue Dancourt. Opening the gate, striding along the passageway, entering the building on the left. She could see him going up to the sixth floor in the tiny run-down elevator. His key in the old ramshackle lock. She didn't want to see what happened next. But the images swung back at her. It was impossible to make them disappear. She had to give in to them, huddled up, holding her breath. They finally left, like a storm moving on. How could she put an end to her loneliness? She had no idea. She didn't feel like knocking at the doors of the other artists in the residence, introducing herself. She wasn't up to it. She remembered that young student who had written to her. Mia White. She hadn't answered her yet. Was meeting her a good idea?

Clarissa's flat still seemed empty, incomplete. Jordan and Andy had found it beautiful. "Slightly inhospitable, don't you think?" Jordan had said cautiously. "Not quite 'you.'" Her daughter had gazed at her keenly, with a speck of concern. She had asked her several times if all was well. Jordan was always worrying about her mother. Clarissa had said yes, of course, everything was fine. Yes, she slept badly. That was just settling into a new home. No, she hadn't yet gotten to know the other tenants of the residence. Just a few of them in the lobby. She'd changed the subject, asking her daughter about her job. Jordan was a hydrologist, working for a major research center on flood risk management.

Jordan had always been essential to her. Even more so since the breakup. Clarissa didn't express this out loud, but she was aware deep down of how much she needed her daughter right now. Jordan had captured the best of both her parents, Clarissa felt. Physically, she had inherited her father's dark hair, his green eyes; she had her mother's startling height, her powerful yet graceful shoulders. She had Toby's kindness, his interest in other people. She had Clarissa's belligerence, her sense of humor. But she was also very much herself: both clever and dreamy, tolerant and yet demanding. You couldn't fool Jordan. She was shrewd and highly intuitive. Clarissa knew that one day, she'd have to tell her about why she'd left François. It was too early. She couldn't face it.

As she prepared a quick lunch in her new kitchen, she listened to Jordan, with the cat perched on her knees, discuss her latest conference. Climate change continued to wreak havoc on meteorological conditions, producing torrential rains, which regularly caused all the rivers of the country to rise. Jordan's specialty was inundation. She worked closely with meteorologists in order to develop preventive strategies for the most vulnerable regions. As a child, she had always been fascinated by water, especially rivers and lakes. Clarissa admired her daughter's expertise and enthusiasm. Jordan was a respected figure in her field. She gave talks, lectures, was often seen on television. She spoke eloquently, with a husky voice that added to her charm.

Clarissa sometimes thought Jordan's profession stemmed from her own interest in quantifying land and premises. In another life, she had been a property surveyor. It wasn't water she used to measure, but houses and apartments. From an early age, Clarissa felt she needed to understand the lay of the land. Her dad had given her a luminous world globe for her desk when she was seven, and she'd spent hours watching it rotate under her finger. Later, she'd developed a fascination for maps, papering the walls of her rooms with them. It was cities she'd found captivating as a teenager: how they emerged, how they expanded, how they were destroyed by fires, bombings, how they were rebuilt. She'd pored over ancient photos of London to see what neighborhoods looked like before the Blitz. In her early twenties, she'd walked around with a measuring tape tucked away in her pocket. Houses attracted her— their stories, their evolution. Her mother had been convinced that Clarissa was going to become an architect. But she hadn't.

While she paid attention to her daughter, slicing bits of mozzarella cheese that Andy promptly put into her mouth despite her grandmother's remonstrance, Clarissa could not help thinking of her firstborn, and what he would have looked like today. He would have been forty-six. Tall and dark, she supposed. But that was all she could conjure. She had not thought of her son for so long, had banished the sorrow to the back of her mind. Her newfound fragility had resurrected it, nurturing it back to a throbbing vitality she found impossible to combat.

When she had started hypnotism, all those years ago, to keep the pain at bay, to not let it destroy her, Elise, her hypnotherapist, had asked her to think of a soothing, restful image. The first thing that had come to mind was a lake. Elise had asked her to describe the lake. Why a lake? She had no idea. She simply knew that the image of the lake soothed her, instilling a prodigious calm into her veins. She had tried to describe the lake to Elise; it was vast, she had the feeling it was deep, and its depth did not worry her. On the contrary, the fact that it reached so amply into the earth, forcing its path into the ground, gave her an unprecedented reassurance. The lake's surface gleamed silver, its smoothness burrowed by steady wavelets. Clarissa could see herself soaring above the lake like a glider, arms outstretched; she could feel the cool wind nip at her cheeks and slide down her back; then she could also discern herself swimming, diving into the watery green abysses, palms stroked by the strange caress of weeds. It seemed to her the lake absorbed her pain, her sorrow.

She often dreamed of the lake. In the middle of the night, when she couldn't sleep, she sometimes asked Mrs. Dalloway to display lake videos on her bedroom ceiling. Half-asleep, she let herself be carried off by eddies, lulled by soft splashing. She didn't know where the water would take her. A peculiar, lacustrine ballet whirled her away; her skin becoming scaly, fishlike, her fingers merging to form pink fins.

In the blue opaqueness at the bottom of the lake, hazy shapes emerged, hands reached out toward her, while spools of black hair slowly unraveled like flowers of darkness, both soothing and poisonous. Once, she thought she caught a glimpse of Virginia Woolf's face—not the face she knew, not the writer's, no, another one, a face that not many had laid eyes upon; the unbearable, bloated, ashen features of the drowned woman, the one whose body had been found weeks after she disappeared on the banks of the river Ouse. The dream of the lake had become a nightmare. It was impossible to know if the images had been born in her own head, or if they came from Mrs. Dalloway's projections.

As she listened to Jordan, Clarissa delicately stroked her granddaughter's head. Adriana, going on fifteen, applied her makeup carefully and wore lacerated black clothes. Despite the rebellious sulk she was fond of sporting, Andy adored her grandmother. She wanted to come and spend the night here. She had even picked out that little couch in the office where she was going to sleep. She interrupted her mother incessantly in order to obtain a date. Jordan got angry. Well, yes, Andy was going to be able to come! Could she just please let her grandmother settle into her new flat? And could she stop being so insistent? Clarissa felt flattered. She, too, loved the relationship she had crafted with her granddaughter.

"Doesn't François live with you anymore, Mums?" Andy asked straightforwardly as Clarissa served them homemade cake for dessert.

Jordan glared at her. Clarissa had been expecting this from her outspoken granddaughter. She calmly replied that no, François wasn't going to live here. This was her place. Only for her.

"And for me!" quipped Andy mischievously.

"That's right, sweetie, for you, too."

"And what about Granddad? Will he come?"

Jordan sighed. Why was Adriana asking these dumb questions? Clarissa smiled, to show them she wasn't ruffled. She reminded Andy that Toby had started over, that he lived in Guéthary, in the Basque country, and that he had a new lady friend.

"Yeah, and she's not much fun," mumbled Andy, helping herself to more cake. "I liked the previous one better. She was less of a pain in the ass."

Clarissa and Jordan laughed. Despite everything, Clarissa had kept up a good relationship with her first husband. Even if they had divorced over thirty years ago, Toby remained close. Which got on François's nerves. Clarissa planned to invite Toby for a drink when he was next in Paris. Without the new lady friend.

"How are things with your brother, Mums?" asked Jordan as she stroked the cat.

Clarissa shrugged. What an idiot, seriously! Her brother! Her laugh sounded pinched and dry. Heritage stories often made a mess of things. She'd always thought she had been close to Arthur.

He was only two years younger than she. They grew up together, spent their childhood and teenage years in London. He did as he pleased. At sixteen, he dressed as Ziggy Stardust, with full makeup, orange hair, and platform soles, to their unadventurous mother's dismay. Their dad found it funny.

"He sounded so cool when he was young!" exclaimed Andy.

"Indeed. But with time, you see, Arthur turned into a full-of-himself, sad little man."

"You bet! And my cousins are no better," added Jordan.

Clarissa didn't have to explain to Jordan and Andy how crushed she had been by Aunt Serena's recent legacy. She'd thought the old lady had been fond of her, just as fond as Serena had been of Arthur. She had often spent holidays in Serena's house in Surrey, with Toby and Jordan, when her daughter was a child. Warm, joyful moments. When the will had been read out loud to her, she had been flabbergasted. Serena had left her entire fortune to Arthur's two daughters, Emily and Harriet. All of it. There hadn't been a single item for Jordan, not even a trinket, a bracelet, or a small souvenir. Arthur's daughters were in for a considerable sum. They'd be able to buy a small flat, go on a trip, invest, plan for the future. Clarissa had felt shock at first, and then uncertainty. Was this a mistake? she'd asked. She was told not at all. A slow, powerful rage replaced the incomprehension. She had called her brother. She still trusted him then; she still hoped. He was going to say, What an old bitch. How dare she do that! He was going to say his daughters would split everything with Jordan. But nothing happened that way. She'd had a hard time getting hold of Arthur. And when his puffy face finally showed up on her screen, he had acted cowardly and evasive. He didn't wish to interfere. Serena had her reasons. They had to respect her decision.

Clarissa had taken the bull by the horns. She had gone to see her nieces. Emily and Harriet hadn't minced their words. They needed the money. They were sorry for Jordan. But they were convinced Jordan had done quite well for herself, hadn't she? They saw her on TV, on social media; she traveled; she seemed to lack nothing; she had a husband and a daughter; her mother was a respected writer. And on top of all that, she was beautiful. Jordan had it all, right? Oh, and one last thing: Jordan had chosen to live in France; one mustn't forget that. Serena was very attached to her country. It was important to her. They had stayed in England, they had no husband or children as of yet, and time was flying by! That money was perfect timing, and they were sure Jordan would understand. What about another cup of tea, dear Aunt C . . . ? Clarissa had felt like strangling them. Her father, who always spoke his mind, was right; he called them tarts. In the train on her way back from London, Clarissa thought about the way Jordan raised Andy, how much effort she put into it, and how complicated it had been during her numerous trips when Andy was a little girl. Clarissa had helped out a lot. What on earth had gotten into old Serena's head? She knew her aunt hadn't approved of the fact that her own brother had married a Frenchwoman. Solange, Clarissa and Arthur's mother, had apparently found it difficult to find her way into her husband's family. Clarissa thought she had ultimately managed to do so. Perhaps not, in the long run.

That day on the train, Clarissa decided she wouldn't be speaking to her brother and nieces again. It was common, after all, to bicker in the aftermath of wills. What was less common, she felt, was the sudden and intimate overlap of every aspect of her life: the breakdown of her marriage, the rough patch with her brother, and the hurried arrival in a new home she still didn't feel at ease in.

When they left, Jordan told her mother to look after herself, to get a good night's sleep, to rest. Andy hugged her with all her might. Clarissa waved good-bye to them as the transparent glass elevator whooshed them down. Jordan's lovely face was turned up to her, and she could read all the anguish there. She knew Jordan was going to speak to her husband, Ivan, tonight, and she already knew what her daughter was going to say: that Clarissa looked old, frail, and sad, that she was worried, that she couldn't understand what had happened. She could hear Jordan's voice: Yes, the flat was lovely, and it was wonderful that Clarissa lived there, but the move had tired her. How was she going to face all this, alone, at her age, in her state? Jordan would undoubtedly bring up the long depression Clarissa had endured after the death of her first child. Jordan remembered that endless tunnel; she was only a little girl at the time, but she had grown up with that despondency. She'd say she feared Clarissa might plunge into a similar gloom. Clarissa could now hear Ivan's voice. Jordan's husband was a tall, thin man in his early forties, with soft blue eyes. He rarely lost his temper and spoke gently but firmly. She could hear him say Clarissa was a tough cookie. She'd pulled herself out of depression a long time ago. Clarissa knew what she wanted. And if Clarissa wanted to be alone, then that was fine. Jordan just had to stop worrying.

Clarissa closed the door of the apartment. She turned her back to it, leaning against the wooden surface, looking out toward the living room. It did look nice, she admitted. The lovely gleaming surfaces. The light. The view. Her precious books, the ones she read with such delight, were missing. They were still at François's. She was going to take the time to make sure they were all placed properly on the shelves. Romain Gary. Virginia Woolf. Her favorite writers. Books never let you down. They were always there for you.

The cat pranced along, and she watched him go toward the main window. Chablis had spent most of the lunch on Jordan's knees, purring. He had eaten well, had played with Adriana. Perhaps he was getting over his apprehension. She was happy about that. She still wasn't quite sure how to deal with a cat. As Clarissa observed him, Chablis suddenly seemed to stiffen. Surely she was imagining things. No, he arched his back, and his ears were flattened, golden eyes deepening to black. The cat crouched now, tail slowly twitching, staring at the middle of the room as if someone were standing there. Mystified, Clarissa remained motionless. He then slunk under the sofa, and the only thing she could see now was the tip of his tail.

Clarissa strode to the center of the room, unnerved, glancing around her. Everything seemed in place, perfectly normal. But she, too, had sensed a presence. And she realized now, with a prick of horror, that ever since she had moved here, she had never felt completely alone; it was as if someone, or something, was watching her.

"Mrs. Dalloway?" She was surprised to hear her voice was quavering. She sounded like a very old lady.

"Yes, Clarissa?" came the rounded, cordial tone.

"Am I alone here?"

"Yes, Clarissa. Apart from the cat, you are completely alone."

"Why was the cat afraid just now?"

"I have no idea, Clarissa."

"Who can see me?"

"I'm sorry, I don't quite understand. Can you rephrase that, Clarissa?"

"Can anyone see what I am doing in my apartment?'" Now her voice was angry. No more quavering old-lady stuff.

"No, Clarissa. No one can see what you do in your home."

"What about you, Mrs. Dalloway? Can you see what I'm doing?'"

"Yes, Clarissa. I see everything you do. I was programmed to do that."

"So you do watch me, Mrs. Dalloway."

"Yes, Clarissa. All the time."

"And so I was right. There is someone spying on me. You."

"You're right, Clarissa. But remember, I'm no one. I don't exist."

Clarissa often thought back to the day she'd spent at the C.A.S.A. headquarters in order to set up her virtual assistant and to meet Dr. Dewinter. She had been shown to a different part of the building, deep down, below ground level. The space here was white and brilliant, almost too white, she thought. The staff wore black as well, the same sleek style as Clémence Dutilleul's suit. The man who took her in charge was in his early twenties. He had the round pink face of a choirboy. His name was Quentin. He was respectful and pleasant. He started by taking an imprint of her fingertips and a scan of her retina with a small device. It took only a couple of minutes. He then told her the setup process was going to take a while, because they needed to get it just right. Even if the questions seemed repetitive and weird, she had to stick to it. The virtual assistant had to get used to her voice, because Clarissa's voice was the only one it was going to obey. It wouldn't respond to anyone else. He also said that Clarissa could take a break whenever she wanted. She could get up, stretch her legs, have a glass of water.

Quentin ushered her into a smaller room, equally white and luminous. In front of her were a chair and a desk. A large screen took up the entire wall. Quentin motioned for her to be seated. He carefully placed earphones on Clarissa's ears. Then he went to sit behind a partition. She could hear his voice in her headset. He asked her if she was ready. She said yes.

The screen in front of her turned gray. Two large eyes faced her now. They were wide and blue. They blinked slowly. They reminded her of the billboard horn-rimmed eyes of Doctor T. J. Eckleburg in the opening pages of *The Great Gatsby;* a solemn, intense gaze, which saw everything, never missing a beat, both reassuring and alarming. An amiable male voice, which was not Quentin's, asked her to say her name out loud. She did so. She was asked to speak more slowly and to repeat her name three times.

In the beginning, it was easy. She had to state her date and place of birth, her nationality. Her age, her height, her weight. The eyes blinked and glowed back at her like those of a gratified cat. Then she had to pronounce a sequence of specific orders. She was asked to repeat them clearly, over and over again.

"Lock the door. Set the alarm. Check the air-conditioning. Turn on the shower. Close the blind. Turn off the light. Set night mode. Turn on the oven. Read my emails."

She was asked to choose the name of her assistant. She had thought about this before, of course. When she said, "Mrs. Dalloway," she then had to say it out loud six or seven times very clearly. She then had to choose what kind of voice she wanted Mrs. Dalloway to have. They could clone any type of voice, she knew. She picked a British accent with mellow, gentle tones.

Quentin appeared from behind the screen. He told her he was going to leave the room. He'd be right outside. She was alone with the setup process. If there was a problem of any sort, she just had to press the pause button. Clarissa nodded. He left, closing the door behind him.

Clarissa felt slightly apprehensive. She remained silent, straight-backed on her chair.

The billboard eyes gleamed back at her.

"Are you ready, Clarissa?" asked the new female voice with the very British accent.

"Yes," she said, "I am."

"Please relax, Clarissa."

"How can you tell I'm tense?"

"Your body language. You don't have to sit up so stiffly. And you can uncross your arms."

Clarissa couldn't help smiling.

"There. That's better. I'm going to be asking you all sorts of questions. Do not be surprised. This is just for me to get to know you better. After all, I will be with you all the time. I need to be able to watch over you. As soon as you walk into the C.A.S.A.

like a mortally wounded beast, a colossal sentry still shimmering with thousands of lights, crashing down amid the excruciating screech of twisted steel. She had asked Arthur and Jane what had happened. How was this possible? Dazed, they hadn't answered. Arthur clicked from channel to channel, hypnotized by the same footage shown yet again, the Tower bending over in that almost grotesque fashion, barely believable, like in a video game or a movie. Clarissa had gone to the kitchen; she'd had a long drink of water, and then she'd turned the radio on. She'd had enough of the uninterrupted contest of pictures displayed on each network; she needed to understand. Again, she tried calling Jordan, Ivan, François. Voice mail. She was terrified. She felt weak. She focused all her attention on the calm voice on the BBC.

She told Andy that she knew then she'd remember that moment for the rest of her life: the vision of her naked feet on the tiles, the brutal heat of that summer night, her hands trembling. The calm voice had gone on to list the facts. Clarissa wondered how could it remain so serene as it proceeded to utter horror after horror. The events in Paris were cataclysmic, said the newscaster very clearly. Clarissa remembered that word: *cataclysmic*. She felt fear pervade her, shoot through her veins like a toxic drug. There was only one name on her mind, her daughter's. She kept repeating it: Jordan. Jordan. Jordan. Nothing could happen to Jordan. Nothing could happen to her daughter.

The calm voice persisted, stirring her. At eleven o'clock French time, in Paris, while the Tower was still shimmering, as it always did upon the hour for five minutes, a large blast occurred at the top of the south pillar, on the level of the Tower's first floor. The origin of the detonation was still not clear, but according to terrorism specialists, it was possibly drones, rigged with explosive devices, driven into the south pillar at a precise spot. No one had noticed the drones making their way through the darkness.

It had taken less than seven minutes for the Tower to fall, time enough for thousands of cameras and smartphones to capture the unbelievable pictures. The Tower toppled over toward the south, flat onto the recent Olympic site built especially for the games, jam-packed with pedestrians on a warm summer evening. But that wasn't all. Within the forty-five minutes of pandemonium that ensued, the voice went on, while firefighters and police had barely gotten under way to rescue the people trapped within the Tower and underneath it, and while many casualties were already feared, a second deadly attack was perpetrated on the same area by more drones. Making the most of the darkness, the small aircrafts dropped three powerful bombs on the sector.

As she stood listening, shaking, horrified, Clarissa hadn't at first noticed her phone was vibrating in her hand. It was Toby. He was calling from his home in the Basque country. He had just seen the ghastly news. He was overjoyed to hear she wasn't in Paris. But he hadn't heard from either Jordan or Ivan. Had she? With dread, Clarissa said she hadn't heard. She hadn't been able to get through. She hadn't been able to get hold of François, either. Toby did his best to reassure her. He kept reminding her that Jordan and Ivan lived near the Bastille, on the east side of Paris. And as for François, he was no doubt safe as well, in their flat near the Luxembourg Gardens. Clarissa listened, nodded, but dread gnawed at her. Ivan had wanted to stay in Paris for the Olympics. Perhaps they had gone to one of the events this past evening, like many Parisians. She couldn't bear to think about it. She felt physically ill. After saying good-bye to Toby, she feverishly perused Jordan's social media posts, trying to check the last time her daughter had been online. She couldn't face going back into the living room, watching the television until morning. It was already getting on to two o'clock. Three o'clock in Paris. She paced up and down the kitchen, cradling the phone to her. She tried calling, again. Again. She kept thinking, I've lost one child in my life. I cannot, I will not, lose another. I will not lose Jordan.

All those years later, she did not repeat those words to Adriana. She had never mentioned her son to her granddaughter. She went on with her memories of that night, telling Andy how it had taken ages to get hold of Jordan and Ivan. The wait was agonizing. The sun came up on another scorching day. It had been impossible to get through to Paris. Telecommunications were down. A part of the city had been irremediably destroyed. She had taken a shower, gone out to buy some bread. People in the streets were stunned, riveted to their phones. London had gone strangely quiet, and it felt like a lull before a storm. François had managed to call from a landline. She felt relief when she heard his voice, but as she had not yet heard from her daughter, the distress was still there. She wanted to leave now, rush to take a train, a plane. She became frantic. A sort of panic came over her. Her brother told her to wait. There was nothing else she could do. She refused to watch TV. She stuck to the radio, sat in the kitchen with a glass of water. The voices described utter chaos. Thousands of people had been killed. Who had perpetrated this? How had it been done? No one knew for sure. At last, just as she had given up hope, Toby called, much later, with the good news. Jordan and Ivan were safe, with Andy, at home. She had broken down and wept.

It had taken a few days for her to be able to get back to Paris. The capital had been on lockdown. She finally returned on a jam-packed train. The city was coated with powdery black dust. Intensified by broiling heat, the acrid, stuffy atmosphere was stifling. Clarissa told Andy that the Olympic Games had been canceled. All the athletes had been told to go home. In her neighborhood, near the Luxembourg Gardens, nothing had changed, on the surface. But the attack could be glimpsed in people's gazes, expressions, and stances. Tourists had fled; they wouldn't return for a long while. She hadn't wished to see the crater left by the bombings; it was splashed over every screen. There was no way to escape it. But her past profession as a property surveyor caught up with her, and the yearning to apprehend the lay of the land, the configuration of places, egged her on. She wanted to see it; she wanted to understand. She waited for as long as possible. A few months went by. She was aware that such widespread damage couldn't be dealt with speedily.

She had gone there on a rainy day, at the end of autumn. High metallic fences hemmed in the entire area. She drew closer, near the ruins of the École Militaire, and had a look. It took her breath away. The damp stench of muck and plaster wafted up toward her. An enormous chasm gaped open below her, enfolded by demolished edifices. Crumbling walls still bore traces of wallpaper, unsteady doors absurdly hanging on hinges, flights of stairs spiraling into nothingness. The immensity of the urban wasteland overwhelmed her. The large boulevards dotted with linden and chestnut trees that she so clearly recalled were now reduced to mountains of rubble lining a bottomless pit. In the distance, the tortured vestiges of the Tower seem to twist with agony toward the drizzling sky.

"Mums, look!" cried Andy. "The hologram! We mustn't miss it!"

The moment had arrived. They both dashed to the living room, opening the main window. They leaned out as far as they could over the railing, the evening air fresh on their faces. High up above, a brilliant light juddered, a lone star glowing in the dark blue sky. The star seemed to dance, flickering like a fairy or a butterfly, and as they watched, a contour slowly flourished below it, drawing a familiar, beloved silhouette all the way to the ground in bold iridescent strokes. The Tower's outline materialized through the darkness, like a divine apparition, as nearby crowds applauded and cheered. Hundreds of people were watching from their windows, as well. It was as if the sparkling Tower had always been there, the powerful beacon shooting from its crown like that of a lighthouse, exactly like it used to. Andy let out a cry of surprise.

"It looks so real!" she said, elated.

Clarissa had to admit that, yes, it did. She reached out to hold her granddaughter tight. Andy was too young to remember the terror in the aftermath of the attack. Later, there was a message from Jordan to her mother. She had finally decided to watch the event; it had given her a sort of hope, the sense of a page being turned at last. Andy asked if she could sleep in the big bed with Clarissa. She didn't want to be alone in the little office. Clarissa had teased her.

"You look worried about something, missy."

"No, I'm just tired."

They had gone to bed before midnight, after a cup of hot chocolate for Andy. It was strangely reassuring to hear someone breathe and move next to her. Clarissa, as always, found it difficult to drop off. She remembered what Jordan had said when her application to the C.A.S.A. residence had been accepted. Had it been a good idea to live in a place where so much suffering had occurred? She suddenly realized she had moved into a dwelling she had never seen beforehand. She had been shown a couple of photos, and that was it. How could she have taken that risk? The irony was that, for so long, her job had been to assess and evaluate apartments for future occupants. She wasn't going to have any regrets. Ever.

"Are you awake, Mums?"

Andy's voice whispered through the dark.

"Yes, my angel. Why aren't you asleep?"

"Too much stuff on my mind. Sometimes thinking stops me from sleeping."

"Story of my life."

"What do you think about?"

"I try not to. I empty my head; I visualize an immense lake, a thick forest."

"I would have loved to have known the world the way it was before. The way it was when you were young. A world with bees, birds, flowers. A world we hardly see nowadays."

"I understand."

"Today's world is so ugly."

"Andy, you sound like a glum old lady."

"I don't care, Mums. Check it out! I don't need to spell it out for you. Look at our situation! Look at where we're heading! Do you think it makes anyone happy? Look at what's happening to the planet. Look what we did to it. Look what's left of the forests. Can you believe I only saw snow once in my life? Heat waves, floods, hurricanes, pollution. And that awful president! People like her have power, all over the world. Look what happened to the Tower, to Venice, to London, to Rome. What are we going to do? Do you see a way out? I don't! I see sod all."

"You need to resist, Andy. Every day."

"Oh yeah? And how?"

"Not thinking like them. Fighting back. Never giving up."

"You say that because you're mature. You know all the stuff I don't. And when you were my age, did you have any idea of what you wanted to do? I have no inkling. And that scares me. Mummy knew."

"Well, I didn't, either. Not a clue."

"You didn't know you wanted to be a writer?"

"No, not at all."

"What were you like at fourteen, Mums?"

In the dimness, Clarissa couldn't help smiling. She felt her granddaughter's silky hair against her cheek. Reminiscing . . . It was like skimming through a photo album, pausing over a page. Slowly letting emotions flow back. There she was, freckled, lanky, and awkward, the braces on her teeth making her miserable. She told Andy she used to be quite a merry youngster, making her friends whoop. She was a prankster on the phone, mimicking people behind their backs, pulling awful faces.

"Hey, it sounds like you were hilarious! And did you fall in love a lot?"

"I had crushes on guys who never looked at me. And those who made passes at me did not interest me in the least."

"Did you hear that, Mums?"

"Hear what?"

"A weird sound. Like something clicking."

Silence.

"I can't hear a thing. Are you sure?"

"Positive."

Clarissa turned on the bedside lamp.

"I'll go check the kitchen and living room. Maybe it's the cat."

"Look, the cat is fast asleep."

Andy slunk under the sheets.

"I'm scared, Mums."

She looked like a small child, snug against the pillows.

Clarissa padded to the kitchen. Everything was peaceful. She walked around the living room. Nothing seemed out of place.

"Mrs. Dalloway?"

"Yes, Clarissa?"

"Have you detected a break-in or anything unusual?"

"No, Clarissa, I've detected nothing of the sort. All is well. Do you wish to report anything else?"

"No, Mrs. Dalloway."

"Fine, Clarissa."

Back in the bedroom, Clarissa comforted her granddaughter.

"I'm not making all this up, Mums, I promise."

"I believe you, missy. But I saw nothing odd."

Andy nestled close.

"You know, it's weird. I like your place. It's pretty and modern, with an amazing view. But . . ."

"But what, Andy?"

"I know you're going to think I'm crazy, Mums. Oh well. I'll tell you anyway. And maybe this is why the cat is scared, too. Ever since I got here, I've felt like we're being watched. All the time."

❧❧❧

NOTEBOOK

After the shock came anger. I was livid. I nearly pressed on the buzzer bearing our name, shaking with rage, awful words coming to my lips. What a bastard.

My husband had another life. A life I knew nothing about. How long had this been going on? How was it that I had seen nothing, known nothing? Had he been that cautious? Or me that stupid?

I stepped back from the building, still trembling. I wasn't going to wait for him to come back out. I had all the proof I needed. It was all there in front of me.

But curiosity got the better of me. Was this just a place he took women to? Or was there only one woman in particular? A woman he met every week, spoke to every day, slept with?

A woman my husband loved?

I wanted more than anything to know who she was.

Should I have left all this alone? Should I have walked away, never done anything about it, never mentioned it? Should I have done what I did?

I thought about it carefully on my way home. I was going to find out who she was and how long this had been going on.

And then I would decide what to do.

When my husband returned that evening, he was his usual self, amusing and caring. He helped me prepare dinner, chose our wine.

While we ate, I looked around at our apartment. I thought of everything we'd built together over the years, and I felt like crying. It was hard not letting my emotions show. I burned to scream at him, to throw things at him. But I held back.

Who was she? What was her name? How old was she? What did she look like? Did he love her? Where did they meet? How did it start?

At one point in the evening, I asked him if I could use his phone to call Jordan, as I couldn't find mine. He said of course, and he opened it for me. He acted like he had nothing to hide.

I had time to check it. There was nothing suspicious on his phone. No photos, no texts. He was being very careful.

There must be another phone, then, I thought. A phone he hid and used to communicate with her.

Two phones, two apartments, two women.

Such a banal situation, I thought. Such a massive cliché.

How wrong I was.

4

TONGUE

I feel certain I am going mad again.
VIRGINIA WOOLF, March 28, 1941

Perhaps the answer lies in the title of my autobiographical novel, The Night Will Be Calm.
ROMAIN GARY, December 2, 1980

WHEN SHE AWOKE, it was still early. She had a quick shower, noiselessly; Adriana was still asleep, with the cat nestled against her. She decided to buy croissants, Andy's favorite. It would take only ten minutes or so. As she got dressed, she thought back to the other nocturnal conversation she'd had with her granddaughter, just after the clicking noise incident.

"Mums, why are you so angry with François?"

Clarissa had known this was going to come up at one point. Andy was too astute not to guess at what was going on. Clarissa'd had to think carefully about what she was going to say. She realized she had not spoken to anyone about François, about what François had done. She wasn't ready yet, and there were things a fourteen-year-old could not understand. But she felt she had to give some element of truth to her granddaughter. She couldn't stay wrapped up in silence forever.

She had said, "He disappointed me."

"Can you explain why?"

Clarissa had stroked Andy's hair in the dark. Where could she begin? When had it started? *Disappointment* wasn't the right word. It sounded too meek, too nice. What she felt was much more powerful and deep-rooted.

"He hurt me badly."

Andy had reached up to caress her grandmother's cheek.

"I hate him for that, Mums. I really hate him. For whatever he did. And I'm not going to ask what it is. I don't think you'll tell me anyway."

"No, I won't. I can't."

"Do you think you'll ever patch it up?"

"No, I don't think so."

She thought of how she had felt when she stepped into the small apartment. She could still smell the perfume. It made her want to retch.

"You're that angry."

"Yes."

"But you've been together for so long!"

"I know. But at this point in my life, I want to move on without him."

"I understand, Mums. I won't mention him again. I'm here if you ever need to talk. I know you think I'm too much of a kid to understand all the adult stuff. But I know how to listen. You taught me how to do that." Her granddaughter's love safeguarded her, toning down her unhappiness. She had managed to drop off, listening to Andy's soft breathing at her side. This morning, she felt less vulnerable.

Clarissa never took the elevator. She enjoyed tearing down the stairs as fast as she could. It took longer climbing the eight flights back up, but it was part of a grueling routine she stuck to. She was fond of stating that all those steps were her way of staying fit. As she rushed past the fourth floor, a door opened, and she found herself facing a brunette in her forties who was wearing sports gear and waving at her. She slowed down, saying hello in return. Her new neighbor's name was Adelka. She was a painter. This was the first time Clarissa had spoken to another artist from the residence. She had occasionally crossed paths with some of them, but it hadn't gone further than an exchange of nods and smiles.

Adelka went down the stairs with her. She was off to run alongside the Seine. Clarissa had a closer look, taking in her brown eyes, thick black hair, tanned skin. This young woman had a charming air about her. Her voice was musical, her smile attractive.

"What do you think of the residence?" she asked her neighbor suddenly.

They were outside at present. Adelka said she had never lived in a place like this. It was impressive. She had been overjoyed to hear her application had been accepted. Many artists had been turned down.

"And what about you? Are you enjoying it, as well?"

Clarissa didn't hesitate long.

"I'm not sure, to tell the truth."

They were walking toward the river, on the old boundaries of the Champ-de-Mars. Contemporary structures, white and resplendent, now took up the space. The artificial trees were pleasantly effective. A couple of electric cars zoomed silently by. It was a calm, enjoyable spot.

"What do you mean?" Adelka asked. "I know you're up on the top floor. It must be quite something."

"Yes, the view is stunning. It's another matter. I feel like someone is watching me all the time."

The coffee-colored eyes narrowed in on her.

"I get it. But to me, that level of surveillance makes me feel safe. I wasn't safe before. I had a violent husband. He gave me a tough time. He smashed up my art material, when it wasn't my face. I know he'll never be able to set foot in the residence. The bastard is blacklisted!"

She burst out laughing. Clarissa couldn't help joining in.

"I have a persona non grata husband, as well."

"Join the club! And what did yours do to get banished from the residence and from your life?"

"He wasn't the brutal type, like your ex. . . . But . . ."

"You don't have to tell me, you know."

It felt wonderful to talk at last, to open up the dams. This woman knew nothing about her, about her life. Clarissa found it easier to unburden herself to this smiling stranger who was her daughter's age than with her long-standing friends, the ones she hadn't wished to see since the breakup.

"I found out in the most shocking way that he was cheating on me."

Adelka made a face.

"Ouch. Not fun. And what did you do?"

"I left him. On the spot."

"And you ended up here, right?"

"That's right."

"You've been married for a long time?"

Adelka walked swiftly; she had the muscular legs of a sportswoman. Clarissa adjusted her stride, attempting to follow her without panting too much.

"Long enough for me to understand I didn't want to stick around for a single minute more."

"You look like a woman who knows what she wants."

"So do you."

They both grinned.

Clarissa asked her about her art, what themes she was involved in. Adelka replied she was interested in bodies. Not young and lovely ones, but hidden ones, different ones, bodies that had nothing to do with beauty criteria.

"And what about you? You're a writer, I believe?"

"That's right. I'm taking notes right now. I'm exploring language. Written language and how it comes to authors. How we choose our words. How we pick some words and not others . . ."

"How ambitious! I feel bad that I haven't read your books. I'll make up for it."

"Not a problem at all. And I'm not familiar with your art."

"How about coming down for a drink one of these days?"

"With pleasure."

Clarissa said good-bye, watching Adelka run at a vigorous pace toward the Seine. She went to the bread shop to get Andy's croissants. A couple of customers there were enthusiastically discussing last night's hologram display. She hurried home, then patiently waited in the lobby for her retina to be scanned. The gate slid open with a chime, and a mechanical voice stated, "Welcome back to the residence, Clarissa Katsef."

In the hall, she crossed paths with Ben, the residence's handyman, who made sure each installation ran smoothly. He had already dropped by her place to check on her network power. He was a young man in his thirties with a mop of curly red hair. Engrossed in his device, he asked her if everything was functioning properly at home. She said yes, thanked him, and embarked upon climbing the stairs. He seemed surprised she wasn't using the lift. Once she got to her floor, she realized it was getting more and more difficult to take each step. She felt drained and breathless, and had to wait a few minutes to catch her breath. When she felt better, she pressed her index finger to the glass plate on the door. It swung open with a click.

"Hey, Mums! You were away for ages!"

"I went to get you croissants, and I met my charming fourth-floor neighbor."

Andy appeared to be flustered.

"I need to talk to you!'"

Clarissa put the croissants in the oven.

"Mrs. Dalloway, heat the oven to one hundred and fifty degrees, please."

"Right away, Clarissa."

"Something happened!"

Startled, Clarissa turned to look at Andy, who was hopping up and down.

"What's up, missy?"

Andy lowered her voice.

"Mrs. Dalloway talked to me!"

"What do you mean, she talked to you?"

"I was playing with the cat, and I heard her voice!"

Clarissa froze.

"Her voice? And she said what?"

"She asked me how I was, something like that."

"You're joking."

"No, I'm not, Mums, and don't make that face. I nearly had a fit when I heard her. I was kind of scared. So I just stood there and I shut up and waited for you. But she went on chatting to me."

Clarissa remained silent, thinking. What did this mean? She didn't like it. There was something amiss. She felt she was being double-crossed.

Then she said in a clear, forbidding voice, "Mrs. Dalloway, did you talk to Adriana while I was out?"

A slight pause.

"Hello, Clarissa! I obey only you. Remember? I was programmed to do just that."

Andy opened wide eyes and gaped.

"Are you sure, Mrs. Dalloway?"

"Perfectly sure, Clarissa."

"Perhaps you don't recall, Mrs. Dalloway?"

"Everything I say to you is recorded, Clarissa."

"Thank you, Mrs. Dalloway."

"You're welcome, Clarissa. Happy to help."

"What the . . ." began Andy.

Clarissa silenced her with an uplifted finger. Her mind was racing. Did this mean she had to be careful now? Should she watch out? No talking? "They" would hear her, right? She picked up her phone, about to send a text message to Adriana. She stopped. Not a good idea. Wouldn't "they" be able to read her texts, as well? Probably.

Clarissa wondered if she wasn't overdoing things. Since François, she'd been spotting evil everywhere. Andy was watching her, puzzled. Perhaps she thought her grandmother had gone crazy. Clarissa grabbed a piece of paper and a pen. She scribbled a few sentences, wrote them very small, in case "they" could zoom in to see what she had written.

"What are you doing?" whispered Andy.

Clarissa handed her the paper wordlessly.

Don't talk. Don't use your phone. Write down exactly what Mrs. D. said and where you were standing when it happened.

Andy understood instantly. She nodded in silence, took the paper, wrote something carefully, and gave it back.

I was in the living room. She said several things: "Hello, Adriana, did you sleep well?" I said, "Are you talking to me?" and she said, laughing, "Is there another Andy here? I don't think so." Then she said, "Do you like Mums's new home?" and "You enjoyed last night's show, didn't you?" And then because I was silent, she said, "You're not saying anything, Andy. Have you lost your tongue?"

Clarissa read it without a word. She tore up the paper and tossed the shreds into the bin. She said blithely, "How about getting dressed, Andy? We could go for a walk and take the croissants with us."

Once they were out of the residence, Andy shot questions at her.

"Why are you looking so worried, Mums? Why is this Mrs. Dalloway thing getting to you?"

Clarissa didn't want to alarm her granddaughter. She briefly explained that during the setup process, she had been told several times that her virtual assistant would respond only to her voice. She suspected they were telling fibs and felt wary. There was something amiss. And being watched persistently was becoming uncomfortable.

"Can't you turn the Dalloway whatsit off? Put it on pause?" asked Andy.

"I don't think so. That won't stop the cameras from filming."

"What if you stuck something onto the cameras?"

"Good point. I hadn't thought of doing that."

They had come to the beginning of the rue de Sèvres.

"I forgot to tell you one last thing, Mums."

"Fire away, missy."

"Mrs. Dalloway spoke to me in English at first, and then in French. Isn't that weird?"

"No, not really; she was programmed to speak to me in those two languages."

Andy swiveled around to look at her grandmother.

"You know what bugged me? It was like she knew me. She knew who I was, knew I was bilingual, knew everything about me."

Later, after Jordan had come to pick up her daughter, Clarissa wandered around the flat with a roll of masking tape. She needed to count the number of surveillance cameras, small black globes in each room. There were ten of them. The only place without them was the small room with the toilet. She decided to get going on the one situated near her bed. She took off her shoes, clambered up on a chair, and stuck a piece of tape onto the black sphere. A sense of freedom surged though her. She never would have thought that being filmed constantly could bother her to such an extent. Why hadn't she reacted when she signed the lease? Perhaps it was time to check.

Installed in the living room, Chablis at her feet, she used her device to pore over the document she'd received when she moved in, as well as the rules of procedure. *Artists are required not to cause any noise: no music or parties after 23 hours. Inebriety will be reprimanded and will lead to discharge after three notices.* Clarissa could not help but smile. Surely that was a bit over the top! She hadn't noticed when she had seen the document for the first time that the names of the other artists were all listed. There were two apartments per floor, apart from the eighth, hers, where she was alone. On the list of names, she made out two sculptors, four painters, five musicians, one poetess, and two writers (herself included). C.A.S.A. offered a messaging service, allowing members of the residence to communicate with one another through a specific channel. She decided to test it.

"Mrs. Dalloway, send an internal message to Adelka, fourth floor, left."

"Of course, Clarissa, go ahead."

"Dear Adelka, I was very happy to meet you this morning. I hope to see you again soon. Your eighth-floor neighbor, Clarissa Katsef."

"I sent it, Clarissa."

"I'm not sure where this messaging service is shown, Mrs. Dalloway."

"You can read your messages on the communication panel situated in the entrance. However, I can read them to you, as well."

"Fine. Please do that when they arrive."

"I've taken note of that, Clarissa."

Clarissa dived back into the contract. It was clearly stipulated that each flat was furnished with a set of cameras "to meet security requirements." She had signed that document. Counterpedaling would undoubtedly prove to be problematic. While she was giving it a thought, Mrs. Dalloway spoke up.

"Clarissa, you've received an answer from your fourth-floor neighbor, Adelka Miki. Should I read it to you?"

"Yes, thank you."

"Here's the message. 'Hello, Clarissa! I was very pleased to meet you, as well. I've just received *Topography of Intimacy,* which I will now start. You see I've wasted no time! What about a drink, end of day, whenever? See you soon. A.' Do you wish to answer?"

"Just say 'Thanks,' and 'See you soon.'"

"It's done."

"Thank you, Mrs. Dalloway."

"You're welcome, Clarissa."

"By the way, please remind me to answer that letter from the bank. For my meeting."

"But you already did answer the bank, Clarissa. Your meeting is next week."

"Really?"

"Do you wish to see a copy of the message you sent? And check your schedule?"

Clarissa had no memory of answering the bank's letter, nor of adding the event to her schedule.

All of a sudden, an insane craving grabbed at her: the urge to abuse Mrs. Dalloway, shooting her mouth off about everything that was on her chest, all that she could no longer put up with. She yearned to scream at the top of her voice, to stamp her feet, to spill her guts. Mrs. Dalloway didn't exist. She wasn't a human being. How would she react? Whatever could Mrs. Dalloway say in order to calm her down, to reason with her? Perhaps she'd stay quiet, after a while. Perhaps she hadn't been encoded to face a string of insults. Clarissa should give it a go, just to see. While she hesitated, the doorbell rang. Mrs. Dalloway announced, "Clarissa, it's Ben. May he enter?"

"Sure, Mrs. Dalloway."

The door opened, revealing the tall, gangly figure wearing white overalls. Ben asked her if an alarm had gone off in her place. She said she'd heard nothing.

"Okay if I check something out?"

"Go ahead."

She followed him into the bedroom. He went straight to the camera covered by the tape and stood in front of it. Clarissa felt as if she'd been caught red-handed. Should she say her granddaughter had done it? Not a clever idea, considering she had been filmed doing the deed herself. Ben was typing something into his device. He remained silent; so did Clarissa. After a while, he extended a never-ending arm and picked the tape off. He turned toward her.

"You're not supposed to stick anything on these." He sighed. "Otherwise, the alarms go off."

She decided to speak up freely. She admitted to him she could no longer bear being monitored, especially in her bedroom. She hadn't taken all this in when she'd signed the contract, and never guessed it would hassle her this way. Ben listened, nodding his head. He seemed in another world. He finally said, "You'll get used to it. It's always like that, in the beginning."

"But who is watching? You?"

"Nope. I just fix stuff that breaks down."

"So, who is?"

"It's for security. No worries."

He asked her if the network was working properly. She said yes. He explained that each flat had its own. Hers was CLARISSA8 and the password was the one they'd chosen together. If ever she needed to change it, she'd have to do it with him.

As he walked toward the entrance, she held him back with a question.

"About my virtual assistant, please?"

"Go ahead," said Ben, his gaze locked on his screen.

She would have liked him to look at her, to pay attention. Arms crossed, she decided to wait until he raised his eyes, surprised by her silence.

"That's better," she said with a sarcastic smile. "I'd like to talk to you about Mrs. Dalloway."

"I'm listening," he said edgily.

"During the setup process, I was told she would react only to my voice."

"That's the case."

"This morning, Mrs. Dalloway spoke to my granddaughter directly. Is that usual procedure, in your opinion?"

"If your granddaughter, or any other person speaks to your assistant, it won't obey that individual. But the assistant may initiate a conversation with someone who happens to be in your home."

"I would rather that not be the case. Mrs. Dalloway doesn't need to intervene with anyone apart from me."

Ben shrugged.

"That can't be modified. All virtual assistants follow C.A.S.A. protocol. Dr. Dewinter can explain that better than me. I have to go, Mrs. Katsef. Anything else?"

Ben went back to his device. She felt like shaking him.

"No. Thanks."

She watched him go with his nonchalant tread. The door closed behind him. She longed to shout "You little asshole!" but the black globes on the ceiling held her back. Could she reasonably hold out in this strange flat where she felt eyes on her at all times? She locked herself up in the small toilet room to calm herself down. Nobody could see her there.

Later on, to get away from the monitoring, she tried shifting the furniture differently in her office. She shoved the desk behind the sofa, so that she could not be seen when she sat to work. While she jostled the table, she hurt her hip. She caught sight of herself in the entrance mirror: wheezing and red in the face. A fit of giggles took over. Seriously, she looked like a lunatic! A madwoman!

Installed at her desk, she felt safe for the first time, a marvelous sensation that made her spirits soar. "They" couldn't see her here, hidden by the back of the sofa. Hands flat out on the table, she breathed in and out calmly, like Elise had taught her all those years ago. This was where she was going to write. This was where she was going to create. This past month had been taxing. Writing would pull her through, the way it always had.

She hadn't looked at her hands for a long time. Stunned, she noticed she was still wearing her wedding ring, the thin golden circle François had slipped on her finger at the town hall in the fifth arrondissement. His name and the date of their marriage were engraved inside it. Despite the passage of time, her hands had remained long and slim, and she slid the ring off easily.

She thought about everything that wedding band had witnessed, seasons, voyages, encounters, lectures, readers, hours of work; simple everyday actions, and the gestures of love: François's body, the number of times her hands had landed on his skin, how it had become familiar to her, like his beauty spots, his carefully groomed beard, his robust neck. The wedding band that had observed every detail of the secret apartment on rue Dancourt.

She found an envelope, glided the ring inside, and placed it in the back of a drawer. A thin white circle remained on her finger, vestige of the jewel she'd worn for so many years, but a sense of liberty blossomed up within her, powering her with an energy she hadn't felt for weeks, to such an extent that she grabbed her notebook, the one she hadn't opened since she got here, a pen, and began to write.

Mia White was waiting for her very nicely, facing number 108, rue du Bac, absorbed not by her mobile, but by a book, an actual book made of paper. She looked like she did in her photos: a lovely young girl with long chestnut hair, wearing jeans, a jacket, and sneakers. Before she went up to her, Clarissa observed her; Mia White seemed captivated by what she was reading, holding her book to her face as if it were a treasure she could not possibly relinquish. The pavement was somewhat narrow in front of Romain Gary's last home, and the young girl had to regularly step back in order to let pedestrians by, but even when she did that, she never took her eyes off the page. What was she reading with such interest? Clarissa drew nearer. It was a vintage edition of *Promise at Dawn,* a paperback that had been read over and over again, lent, lost, found, with warped pages and a torn and tattered cover, everything Clarissa loved: a well-thumbed book.

"Oh! It's you!"

So Mia White had spotted her. What a smile!

"You're bang on time," said Clarissa in French.

"I'm the punctual type," said Mia White, speaking in French, as well.

They turned around to face the large pale building behind them.

"So it was here," said Mia White.

"Yes, here. But no need to get emotional looking up at those second-floor windows. Romain Gary's place gave on to an inner courtyard."

They crossed the street to get a better view.

"I'd like to know . . ." Mia White paused in mid-sentence, shyly.

"What?"

"That scene, in *Topography of Intimacy,* about Gary's apartment. Did it really happen that way? The way you wrote it?"

"More or less."

"I loved your book, but I especially loved that bit."

Clarissa searched the young girl's face. Mia White seemed perfectly sincere. Her magnificent eyes, riveted to Clarissa's own, brimmed over with discernible esteem. It had been a while since anyone had looked at Clarissa that way. It felt good.

"Would you mind telling me again how it happened? It would be such an honor."

Mia White spoke in English this time. Not that it made any difference to Clarissa. She knew all too well how true bilinguals were incapable of sticking to one language; they switched from one to the other with astounding changeability, making interlocutors who didn't have the possibility to express themselves seamlessly in two languages feel giddy. Mia White had no accent in either French or English, like herself.

Clarissa pursued in English, pointing to the building. She told Mia she had first come to 108, rue du Bac several years after Gary died. She had just moved to Paris, after spending her childhood, her adolescence, and her university years in England. She worked as a property surveyor for a notary office and a real estate agency. She lived on rue d'Alésia, with the young man who would soon become her first husband. She had no idea the writer Romain Gary had committed suicide here on December 2, 1980. Her colleagues and she were to assess an apartment on the third floor. While they worked, the writer became the topic of their conversation.

Clarissa knew nothing about Gary. One of her associates was familiar with his life story. Clarissa was captivated by the flamboyance of his existence: Born Roman Kacew in Lithuania, the only child of an impassioned and whimsical mother, he became, in turn, an aviator, war hero, writer, diplomat, and filmmaker. He moved into number 108 in 1963, with his wife, the American actress Jean Seberg. He had lived there for nearly two decades. As Clarissa listened, her inquisitiveness had grown. In those days, the late eighties, with no Internet and no Google, she reminded Mia White, smiling, books were still purchased in bookstores. That evening, she had gone to buy *Promise at Dawn*. The title had enticed her. Looking at the back cover, she discovered a man with thoughtful features, startlingly clear eyes, a well-drawn mouth. At that point, books didn't have such a large part in her life. She wasn't yet the reader she would later become; she read seldom, and slowly.

It had taken her a while to immerse herself in Romain Gary's realm. She bought other books, *The Roots of Heaven, White Dog,* and *The Life Before Us,* which he had published under another name: Émile Ajar. Little by little, Romain Gary's prose had acted upon her like a sort of drug. She had been taken aback by his seductive fusion of delicacy and potency. His writing, both poetic and brutal, appealed to her. She had been expecting the ascetic and irreproachable works of a grand intellectual; instead, she stepped into the teeming world of a creative virtuoso who had never ceased to reinvent himself. Who was Romain Gary? All his life, he excelled in the art of covering his tracks. A young author, Dominique Bona, had just published the first biography concerning him. Clarissa had devoured it.

Clarissa crossed the street again, with Mia White following her, over to the iron fence enclosing number 108. She placed her palm on the handle. She said in French, "I needed to come back here regularly, especially since I'd read his books. I was following in his footsteps, setting my hand where he'd set his over and over again, like an intimate pilgrimage."

"I understand," said the young woman solemnly.

"You don't find it morbid?"

"No. Not at all. It's like paying tribute to him."

There was curiosity mingled with admiration in Mia White's scrutiny. Clarissa took up with her story. One morning, as she was passing by, some time after the measuring of the third-floor flat, she noticed the gate of number 108 was held open by a wedge. She had made the most of it, slipping inside. She hurried to the main stairway, on the right. As she went up the steps, she discovered movers emptying Romain Gary's old apartment on the second floor. The door was half-closed. She had hesitated, fleetingly, on the landing. Since 1980 and Gary's death, she realized, several occupants had probably lived here one after the other. She was not going to walk into a home that still bore his imprint, as his furniture, paintings, and books were no longer here. But it was the layout of the flat that drew her in, how this man, whom she found mesmerizing, had moved within these very walls, how he had occupied the premises. She put one foot into the entrance. She remembered the third-floor flat measured with her colleagues was L-shaped, 372 square meters, with eight rooms giving on to a tree-lined private lane.

Romain Gary's sixty-six-year-old body had been carried from here, over this threshold, and down the stairs behind her. She moved forward, cautiously at first, then with a firmer gait. If someone asked her what the hell she was doing, she'd say she had made a mistake and ended up on the wrong floor. But no one came. She had remained alone in a string of vast rooms leading one into the next. She noticed the parquet floors had here and there been replaced by charcoal slate tiles, that fireplaces had been removed. A large bedroom overlooked the courtyard and its chestnut trees. She had a gut feeling it had happened here. The bed must have been placed against the wall on the left, between two electrical sockets. A bed made of copper. She'd read that in the biography. He'd lain down for the last time where she was standing now. He had placed his last handwritten letter at the foot of the bed. A note that began with "D-Day. No connection with Jean Seberg." A year before, in 1979, the actress, with whom he no longer lived, had been found dead in her car near avenue Victor-Hugo in Paris, the police ruling her demise a probable suicide. After that, Romain Gary had given up writing for good.

Clarissa's expert gaze, honed by her professional training, scanned the room. The radiator was vintage; so was the door leading into the adjacent bathroom. She passed into it. There had been no recent refurbishments here. She'd read that Gary used to dictate his books to his secretary (and lover) while he took his bath, cigar clamped between his teeth. Romain Gary had looked at himself daily in this very mirror. In this private place, he had washed and groomed himself, had tended to his body and its needs. These walls had witnessed his nakedness.

It felt like he was beside her now, buttoning up one of his custom-made mauve satin shirts, an ornate cabochon ring on his left hand, and he seemed close enough for her to make out the blue intensity of his eyes, his bittersweet smile, and the beard he carefully blackened to wipe out traces of gray. Did she perceive the acrid waft of a Montecristo? Almost. She stood at the heart of his private life, where he had slept, dreamed, and loved; where he had decided to end it all. The perimeter of his death was revealed to her.

Clarissa went on, while Mia White listened attentively. Tuesday, December 2, 1980, had been a rainy day. After lunching with his editor in the neighborhood, and relishing a last cigar, Romain Gary had walked home along the rue de Babylone. He was by himself. He had closed the shutters and the curtains. He had planned it all. He had not faltered. He had done what he had intended to do. Killing himself, in his room. He had taken the Smith & Wesson from its case, spread a red towel over his pillow, and had lain down, the barrel lodged between his lips. No one had heard the gunshot.

Clarissa remained quiet for a while.

"When I read that part in your book, I felt like I was there with you," whispered Mia White.

Clarissa continued. She had looked at the ceiling for a long moment, which must have been the last thing Gary's eyes had glimpsed. She had wondered, since that rainy afternoon, what Gary had left behind. Those who slept there, in that room, within those walls, had they not been marked, in one way or another, by his bloodstained wake? Without meaning to, Clarissa had picked up the writer's fragility, connecting to his torment, loneliness, and despair; the emotions had engulfed her as soon as she had walked into his old apartment, leaving their stain on her.

"Did Gary transmit a form of gloom to you?" asked Mia White.

"He had already done that through his books. There's this beautifully melancholic quote in *The Life Before Us*: 'It's always in the eyes that people are the saddest.' I experienced a special connection with him that day on rue du Bac."

"Did you already know you were going to write about that moment?"

"No," said Clarissa impulsively. "Writing came much later to me, via another angle, via Virginia Woolf and what I felt when I visited her home. But the fascination with this place, for this room, has never left me. Telling you this story all these years later revives it all."

The two women were now walking up the rue du Bac toward the Seine. Mia White's long chestnut hair rippled in the light breeze.

"Are you working on a new book?" she asked.

"More or less. I haven't gotten very far because of my move."

"Which area did you move to?"

Her beguiling smile. Her wide blue eyes.

The small inner voice murmured: *Never get specific with a reader, remember, nothing about where you live. Cloud the issue. It's okay to lie. Don't give any indications, addresses, street names.*

"I'm in the new district, at the top of avenue Gustave-Eiffel, near the Tower Memorial."

Too late.

"Oh, I never would have thought you'd choose to live there! I thought you didn't like modern buildings."

"On the contrary, it's a nice change, being somewhere brand-new. No one's lived there before me."

"You like it, then?"

Don't tell her about Mrs. Dalloway, about the cameras, about the spooked cat. Shut up.

"Very much so."

Mia White was shorter than Clarissa. She moved gracefully. Pedestrians often turned around to stare at her, Clarissa noticed. They strolled along the river, toward Île de la Cité. Clarissa asked her if she'd made some new friends. The young girl said she'd met a couple of nice people. She missed her boyfriend. He lived in England. They saw each other every other weekend.

The conversation became slightly idle. Time was ticking by. Clarissa knew one should never spend too much time with a reader. At times, they became inquisitive, asked too many questions, turned out to be clingy. This wasn't the case with Mia White. She seemed to be enjoying Clarissa's company, and nothing more. Clarissa asked her about her own writing. The young girl blushed.

"How sweet of you to remember that! Yes, I'm writing. But I'd never dare show you anything."

"What language do you write in?"

"For the moment, in English. It's not easy making a choice, when you're bilingual. And yourself?"

"Ah, well, I've decided to no longer make that choice, you see."

Mia White's eyes grew even larger.

"What do you mean?"

"I've decided to write my new novel in two languages at the same time."

The inner voice again. *What the hell are you doing? Why blab about your writing projects with a stranger?*

"How are you doing this? It sounds amazing!" exclaimed Mia White.

They had turned back and were now standing in front of the rue du Bac Métro station. Clarissa could have added nothing more, said good-bye, and departed. She didn't feel like being alone, returning to her silent flat, her fearful cat. This smiling young girl did her good.

"What about a break at that café?" she suggested. Mia White agreed, with pleasure. She ordered a Coke, and Clarissa, some tea.

"What do you speak with your family?" asked Mia White. "Me, it's English with my dad, French with my mum, a mix of both with my sister."

"My first husband is an American, so I spoke to him in English. And to make sure our daughter became bilingual, I always addressed myself to her in French. My second husband is French, but I sometimes speak to him in English, Lord knows why!"

They laughed in unison and Clarissa ignored the annoying inner voice: *What the hell are you doing, pouring your life out? Rambling on about your husbands, how ridiculous!* She was letting go at last. She hadn't chatted with a friend for such a long time.

"I get the oddest questions," said Mia White, and Clarissa noticed for the first time what a pleasant voice she had. "I'm asked what language I dream in. That stumps me. I think about it, and I just don't know. Isn't that strange? What about you?"

Clarissa couldn't bring herself to tell Mia White about her recent dreams. Ever since she had started living in the residence, they seemed more and more vivid. In the past, she'd had difficulty remembering them. Now she didn't have to write the dreams down. Now, when she awoke, they lingered, shadowing her all day long. She kept on hearing the voice as well, the reassuring murmur that whispered to her while she slept. She couldn't recall what it was saying. All she knew was that it meant well. And, come to think of it, she had no idea which language it was using.

"I wish I knew, but I'm like you, I don't have a clue," she said, not wishing to discuss her dreams any further. She wondered if Mia White perceived her hesitancy. "Do dreams have a language, in your opinion?"

"Well, they must. But perhaps, to people like us, our unconscious doesn't decipher language. I'm also asked what I swear in. I had never really noticed that before. But when I paid attention,

I realized it was French. God knows why! And you? Do you prefer cursing in French, as well?"

Clarissa smiled again, but with a touch of bitterness this time. She thought of the expletives that had rushed to her lips while she had been packing her bags, François standing next to her, begging and pleading for her to stay. She hadn't pronounced a single one of them; she had remained wordless, but they stormed around inside her head, loud, blunt, and obscene. English? French? Probably French, because that was François's mother tongue.

She said nothing of all this to Mia White, who seemed to take in every one of her movements and reactions with her intense, unwavering gaze. To escape it, Clarissa looked down at the sunbeam caressing their hands. Mia White's were tiny and golden.

"A mix-up, isn't it?" Mia White said lightly. "And what about your book, then? I'm so curious to know more."

The young woman was waiting for her to speak. For a few seconds, Clarissa stayed quiet, watching the shaft of light playing with her spoon. Then she sprang forth. She said she had never translated her own writing. She had written some books directly in French, others in English. There was invariably a pang of regret from having to choose one over the other. She then worked with translators, a task she often found difficult. Recently, she'd decided to experiment: writing simultaneously in both languages, two documents opened up on her computer, one in English, one in French. It was bewildering at the start, and then all of a sudden, there had been a revelation, acting upon her like a boost, heightening her energy. She had shifted from a quiet country path to a motorway. She wrote her text, no longer paying attention to the language she was writing in. She wrote. That was it. Language no longer mattered. Or rather, both languages now had their significance, because each of them bestowed on her the sentences or words she was seeking, which she then had to transpose with care, perfecting them with the patient and meticulous fine-tuning used on an antiquated receiver, so that the frequency she obtained was the same in English and in French. She perceived herself as a voracious foraging bee harvesting pollen for two separate hives, another pleasing image.

"How amazing!" exclaimed Mia White, dazzled.

Heartened, Clarissa went on. The manuscript was coming along like a two-headed monster, thriving homogenously. She didn't favor one language over the other, and wanted above all for the text to end up identical in both. At times, as she labored over a description, she switched directly to the other language, which instantly gave her a new boost. It was like playing out Jekyll and Hyde in an unprecedented scientific experimentation. Who was Hyde? Who was Dr. Jekyll? English or French? It didn't matter. She wasn't certain she'd go on writing in this way. All she knew was that she certainly didn't regret giving it a go.

"I'm sure you're aware Samuel Beckett wrote in English and French, as well," said Mia White. "And so did Julien Green."

"Yes, that's right. And did you know Romain Gary also translated himself?"

Mia White looked surprised. No, she had no idea. Clarissa explained that Gary wrote *White Dog* in English first, like *Lady L,* and other novels, and then adapted them to French, which was unexpected, considering he was brought up learning Polish and Russian, and that neither French nor English had been his mother tongue.

"His real name was Kacew?" asked Mia White.

"Yes."

"Pronounced like your pen name?"

"That's right."

"Clarissa for Virginia Woolf and Katsef for Romain Gary."

"Yes. I started writing because of those two writers."

"Yes, I read that. I hope you'll tell me about Woolf next time we meet."

"With pleasure."

Oh, come on, said the inner voice. *Because you're going to see her again? Seriously? You're going to go on prattling? You don't know anything about her. You have no idea who she is. You think she's sweet and charming, but perhaps she's none of that. Wake up.*

"This is my mobile number," said Mia White, with her enchanting smile. "I'll let you get back to me."

Later, on the phone, Clarissa told her daughter she had made two new friends. A young reader, barely older than Andy, and her fourth-floor neighbor, with whom she was going to have a drink at the end of the week. Jordan congratulated her, and told her about the brooch belonging to Aunt Serena, sent by Mimsy and Pimsy, which had just arrived.

"It is pretty?"

"Hideous."

"What are you going to do with it?"

"No idea. Sell it? Andy doesn't want it. I'll have it appraised, but I'm sure it's not worth much."

"I'll thank Grandpa and Arthur on my end."

Clarissa hung up after lovingly saying good-bye to her daughter.

She hadn't told Jordan she felt more and more tired, that she still slept badly, that her dreams were beginning to disturb her.

She hadn't told Jordan about the infinitesimal dark zone behind Mia White's luminous smile.

As she made her way to her room along the corridor, she heard a metallic clicking sound. Startled, she stood still. Was this the sound that had frightened Andy?

Then she noticed Chablis.

The cat was frozen to the spot, its fur bristling. Arching its back, it was staring up toward the ceiling, petrified.

NOTEBOOK

I spent some time hanging around in front of the building on rue Dancourt. There was a small café just in front of the passageway railing, from where I could see all the way into the courtyard to the main door.

I knew she was a long-haired blonde. That was all. I had to see her. To see her with my own eyes.

How long had this double life been going on for? I had no idea. I remembered how often my husband had recently been away for business trips. Did she go with him? Did his coworkers know? Who knew anything about this?

I had never checked to see if he really left Paris. I trusted him.

The little café on rue Dancourt was a quiet place. The manager was nice and not too chatty. I always had my notebook with me. I pretended to work, but to tell the truth, I was incapable of writing anything. My eyes never left the railing.

A lot of people passed by there. Day after day, I became familiar with the residents. The elderly lady and her dog. The trim gentleman with his briefcase. A tall and handsome bearded young man. A mother and her teenaged daughter, not speaking to each other. A grouchy old man. A woman of my age with her grandchildren.

I'd see my husband go by with his shopping basket. He'd come back all chirpy-looking, with tarts from the bakery and flowers. I'd watch him, incredulous.

I longed to tear out of the café, run after him along the passageway, insult him and fling his pastries and bouquets into the gutter.

He was always alone. No woman by his side. I waited for a blonde to appear. There was one, but she had short hair and a boyish look. In her thirties. Not his type. But what was his type? I wondered. She seemed tired and fed up. One evening, she was holding a small girl by the hand. I nearly had a fit. My husband had a hidden child! He had never dared tell me. The blonde was his mistress. I remained rooted to the spot. I hadn't known what to do.

A few days later, the blonde went by with a fat, hairy man. He was holding her by the waist, kissing her neck. I sighed with relief. Nothing to do with my husband.

Still no sign of a long-haired blonde. Was she already in the flat? Did she live there? They were never together outside. Was there another entrance? I checked. There wasn't.

I wasn't getting it. All sorts of qualms came over me. Maybe there was no blonde. Just a place where my husband went to be alone. But what about the tartlets, the flowers?

Was this a bachelor pad where he met a string of women? I couldn't quite believe that. He was, after all, getting on.

What was he hiding from me, then? A fling with a man? I felt dizzy.

Writers really have too much imagination.

I had to calm down, to stop spinning stories in my head.

There was only one thing to do. Confront them.

No, better still. Tackle her, without my husband. Deal with her alone. Face-to-face.

5

POWDER

I don't think two people could have been happier.
VIRGINIA WOOLF, March 28, 1941

I have at last said all I have to say.
ROMAIN GARY, December 2, 1980

CLARISSA WAS HAVING her breakfast, and reading the morning paper on her device. For a while now, she'd steadfastly avoided lingering on bad news, attempting to concentrate on what might instruct her, stir or touch her, or even make her laugh. It wasn't easy. The news feed prospered on disasters and cataclysms. She also had to check each time that she wasn't dealing with fake news. She had often been hoodwinked.

Mrs. Dalloway was heard.

"Good morning, Clarissa. We have a situation. A person has tried to come in several times. His name is not on the entry list."

François. It could only be him.

"Is he downstairs, Mrs. Dalloway?"

"Yes. And he won't leave unless he speaks to you. He went away previously, after speaking to security. But not this morning. What do you wish to do?"

"Can you confirm his identity?"

"Of course."

François's shattered face loomed up on the nearby control screen.

"I'll give it a thought, Mrs. Dalloway."

"Absolutely."

Clarissa got up, her mug in her hand. She tried to think rationally. She tried to remain calm. There was nothing she wanted to say to François, except for him to leave her alone. The pain concerning the purple studio was still there, as strong as ever. And now he was downstairs. What was he thinking? That she was going to go back to him? That she would forgive him, like she always had? That she would be the wonderful, generous, understanding wife she had been till now? Oh no. No, no. That Clarissa was gone. Gone forever.

She saw herself in the mirror and almost gasped at the expression on her face. The woman staring back at her was a warrior. It felt as if she were wearing armor, that nothing this man could ever do would hurt her or disappoint her again.

Go on down there, said the little voice. *Give him a piece of your mind. Make him understand, for once and for all.*

She drew herself up to her full height. Then she reached into her cupboard and pulled out a pair of badass black boots she'd bought last week on the spur of the moment, the kind she used to wear when she was younger, and that only a rock star or an actress would ever dare flaunt at her age. They added a couple of inches to her frame, exactly what she wanted.

She had purchased new clothes, as she had moved here with nothing. She was particularly fond of an elegant black jacket, unearthed in a vintage boutique, which contrasted with her red hair. She slipped it on and applied light makeup. She had no intention of coming across as pallid or worn-out. In the bathroom, Mrs. Dalloway asked her to go through the medical procedure: weighing herself, placing her hand on the plaque, looking into the mirror where the dots were.

"Another time. I'm in a hurry."

"Fine, but Dr. Dewinter insists on your going through the evaluations regularly. I will remind you."

Clarissa made a face. Then she mumbled, laughing up her sleeve, "Blah blah blah."

She left, banging the door behind her, hurrying headlong down the stairs, as usual.

François was waiting for her a little farther away on the cobbled forecourt in front of the residence, like a lost, collarless dog. He had the bushy, unkempt beard of a nineteenth-century tanked-up Slavic writer; his face was puffed up, his eyes reddened. His back was curved, his chin glued to his chest. Was he overdoing it, so that she might pity him and relent? It wasn't working. He was pathetic, she thought.

"It's impossible to get into that fortress of yours," he said with a feeble smile.

"What do you want?" she asked bluntly.

His face fell. Then he began to speak hurriedly. What he wanted? Was she serious? He had been here three times already in the past weeks, only to be sent away by those guards, who treated him like a homeless person. He only wanted to talk. He only wanted to make her understand, nothing more than that. He had done something awful, something heinous. He could not forgive himself. But he couldn't lose her. He couldn't let her walk out of his life. He needed her. He had always needed her. How could she turn over this page so fast? After all they'd gone through, after all these years? Couldn't she just hear him out, let him explain? Surely she might let him explain?

Clarissa glanced at his disheveled shirt, his stained jeans. The sour stink of him wormed its way to her nose. This was unlike him. François was usually impeccably groomed. He looked like he hadn't slept or washed in weeks.

He went on in a calmer, plaintive, squeaky voice she found

unbearable. They had to talk about the future, didn't they? They had to make plans. If she really wished to leave, then they had to organize this. She had all her stuff at the flat. There were papers to sign, all sorts of things to do, if she truly wanted to go. Had she thought it over? Was this what she wanted?

She spoke at last. Her voice was clear and firm.

"Yes, this is what I want."

She held herself tall, towering over him in her heels. How could she ever have loved this man who was so small in every single way? Every aspect of him was insignificant. The more she observed him, the more she wondered how it had been possible. How had she fallen in love with François Antoine? She remembered he had appeared at a traumatic moment in her life. She had not gotten over the death of her baby, despite Jordan's birth. Her job as a surveyor was beginning to bore her. It was a complex, tricky period. She had met François Antoine at a mutual friend's place. She had gone to the dinner alone; Toby had moved out long ago. What had she seen in François? There was something comforting and caring about him. It was François who had been the first to ever suggest hypnosis to her; he had sensed her fragility, the sorrow she had still not been able to overcome concerning the child. She didn't have to explain. He suggested she give it a try, just once. And later, much later, that first hypnosis session with Elise Delaporte had changed everything for her.

"You're so tough, Clarissa. So unkind. That's not your style. You've forgotten everything I've ever done for you."

He went on in his lamenting tone. Did she have a short memory, or what? Did she not remember the state she was in when he met her? Her first husband had already cleared off, after all.

"That's enough, François," she hissed.

But he went on with more intensity. Yes, Toby had gotten the hell out because Clarissa was wallowing in her own grief, because she couldn't even smile anymore, let alone to her own daughter.

Did she have any idea what he had endured? Did she even guess at the efforts he'd made to help her picture things in a more positive light, at all the trouble he had gone through to help her heal? Look at how she was treating him now, slamming the door on their marriage.

"Stop it, François. It's over. It's finished."

His face crumpled up, and it was ugly to watch. She thought about the studio, the photos and the videos she had seen there, that hidden, double life. Ugly, as well. It was all so ugly. She didn't want any of it. She could no longer stand it.

"Please give me another chance. Please forgive me."

He was weeping now, his nose runny, his eyes screwed up. Disgust rose over pity. How could she tell him, again, that there were so many things she had put up with, too much she had taken in her stride, so many times she had pardoned. He had been unfaithful since the start. It had been an unpleasant discovery, but not a surprise. She was no young bride. But this was different. This had nothing to do with the previous flings. This was a repugnant blow that had dug into the very core of their marriage, delving into the throbbing heart of it, and there was no going back from that debacle; there was no healing, no possibility of absolution.

He didn't seem to be getting it. He was still crying, his beard flecked with snot. He kept on mumbling that he had been such an idiot; he was so angry with himself.

"I imagine you're still seeing her?" she asked. She felt invincible in her black jacket, perched on her high-heeled rock-star boots. But the pain always found a way to express itself, perfidiously snaking its way through her shield. Why ask such a dumb question? Of course he was still seeing her! He had installed her in a studio; he had a life with her. For a year now, he'd been sharing part of his existence with this creature.

François looked sheepish. He stared at his feet. Words weren't coming to him.

"You know what?" said Clarissa bitterly. "Forget that question. Don't answer. I don't want to know."

"I thought perhaps you might understand," murmured François at last, with the same hangdog expression. "I was mistaken."

She stamped her foot.

"For God's sake, François, what is there to understand?"

He shook his head, raised his hand. Could she just listen? Was that possible? She remained silent. He took that as a cue. He said he had needs, like any man, and she knew that. The problem was, with age, his needs were still strong. He couldn't ignore them. He had to face the facts. They had married late, in their fifties. Then he had been ill. Of course, there had been sex between them, but perhaps not as much as he would have wanted. Maybe he was wrong, but it seemed to him that as she grew older, she seemed to be less interested in sex. Perhaps it was menopause? Perhaps they hadn't talked about it enough? He hadn't dared. He hadn't known where to begin.

Clarissa took a deep breath. She tried to put her anger and disgust aside.

"What are you trying to tell me?" she said.

François seemed to stand a little straighter. He looked her in the eyes. He had been meaning to speak to her, but he just didn't know how. Never could he have imagined she'd follow him and discover the studio. He should have told her right away, and the more he waited, the more difficult it became to say anything. His voice became clearer, less shrill.

"I thought you'd understand because you're so intelligent, Clarissa. You see into people's souls. And I really and truly thought that you wouldn't feel hurt, because you don't give me anything sexual anymore. Nothing much goes on in our bed, except hugs and kisses. I can't even remember the last time we made love. When I'm with her, it is only for that. It's just for the sex. It's only for the sex."

A violent fury took over, and she had to restrain herself from insulting him. She was shaking.

"Oh, really? Only for the sex?" she hissed frostily. "What about the photo albums? The videos? The celebrations? The dinners for two? All in the past year? I saw it, as it's so nicely on display, in your home. Enough of your nonsense. Cut the crap, please. Stop saying she's just some lay. You love her. You know it. You're in love. And it's intolerable. Unbearable."

Like a little boy, he started to cry again.

"I love both of you," he whined; "it's a nightmare. I'm so sorry, honey. Forgive me!"

He blubbered loudly, with no holding back.

Clarissa stepped back, raised her chin.

"You're going to get the hell out of here. Now. You're never coming back. Is that clear? I'll talk to a lawyer when I'm ready. That lawyer will get in touch with you. That's all. Bye."

She rushed away, without looking at him. The scanning system at the entrance had trouble checking her retina because of her tears. She had to go through it several times, praying François wasn't behind her. She climbed the stairs too quickly, and had to stop halfway, breathless, her throat dry.

Mrs. Dalloway's voice greeted her as soon as she walked in.

"Clarissa, tonight on channel Cinéma New Star, there's a special Timothée Chalamet show. Otherwise, there's a Chopin concert on—"

"Just shut up, Mrs. Dalloway. And don't speak to me before tomorrow."

Silence.

A prodigious feeling of freedom raced through her.

In the living room, the cat was curled up on the sofa, asleep. She sat down next to him and stroked his back. He purred. She put François out of her mind. She thought of all the things she had to do. The trick was to keep busy. It was the only way. In her mind, she made little notes. Check on her father to see how he was. Call Jordan to find out if the brooch was worth anything. Start thinking about the summer holiday, the first she'd spend without François. They usually spent them in Provence or Italy. Where would she go? And while she went through all these things, the idea of the book she was trying to write loomed up bigger than the rest. Luckily, the editor she worked with was not breathing down her neck. Laure-Marie knew Clarissa needed time. And Clarissa was well aware that although her books were valued, she was not a bestselling author whose new works were eagerly expected. There was no hype around her, and never had been. No one from the publishing company put pressure on her. It was always a pleasure to have lunch with Laure-Marie, who took her to nice restaurants and seemed genuinely happy to see her. But Laure-Marie had bigger and more important authors to look after.

Perhaps it was time to call Laure-Marie and tell her that she had just started working on something new. She wondered what Laure-Marie would make of the fact that Clarissa was writing in English and French simultaneously. Would she be interested? Perhaps not. Since the attacks, the world of publishing had changed. The dreadful power of the images searing around the world on social media, showing the devastation of the Piazza San Marco, bombed-out Big Ben, and the obliteration of the Sistine Chapel, seemed to have stopped time. After the Eiffel Tower had been filmed crashing down, it had not seemed possible that anything worse could ever happen. And yet it had.

But that was only the beginning. A swift and fiendish sequence of events had occurred. Pictures took precedence over words. No one read newspapers. People watched videos, over and over again, ensnared by an enthralled stupor.

Clarissa recalled that several years after the attacks, during the oddness of an unhoped-for and disquieting lull, while Europe as Clarissa had always known it started to fall apart, and as the bees endured a slow agony worsening by the day, other new and horrify-ing images had spread like an epidemic: Ordinary citizens, unable to stand the cruel reality of modern life, were committing suicide on social media for all to see. Individuals of all ages, all classes, all nationalities posted live videos of themselves taking their own lives, one after the other. It was beyond belief: an atrocious and despotic larger-than-life reality show caught in the frenzy of me-dia display. Literature no longer held its own, faced now with the onslaught of immediacy, where the obscene power of video reigned supreme, never satiated. And when stunned writers had attempted to describe the attacks, those books had barely been read. People preferred to come and listen to the writer, to applaud the writer as he or she read from his or her book, and no lon-ger purchased signed copies. Reading was no longer comforting. Reading no longer helped to heal.

So why should she go on writing? Who would read her? She would stick to writing because she didn't have a choice, because written words were her stronghold, her defense. She would write to make her voice heard; she would continue in order to leave a trail, although she had no idea who'd ever find it. She would write.

Clarissa felt tired, more than ever. It was an effort to get out of bed, to walk up those eight flights of stairs. Why was her mouth so parched all the time? Perhaps she was overdoing things. Perhaps she needed to slow down, write less and with less passion, though that was going to be hard.

One night, as she lay asleep, the voice murmured a word, over and over again, lapping into the breeding ground of her sensitive brain like a recurring wave, never letting go. Like a time ma-chine, the dream was taking her back over the years to a place that filled her with dread. She heard the squeak of wheels on worn linoleum, saw the long stretch of a dark corridor opening up in front of her. She saw Toby, his hair still black, bending down to weep, his face in his hands. The voice whispered the same word that burrowed deep into her, down where she could still feel the soreness, down where she kept the pain at bay. But the voice acted like a key, unlocking all the doors of protection she had so carefully erected, and the suffering came gushing back, stronger than ever, like boiling water scalding her skin. In her dream, she surrendered to the pain, opening herself completely, letting it invade her. The voice was there to calm her, to reassure her. When she opened her eyes, she felt moisture on her cheeks. She had been crying. She felt calm, but desolate, as if something had been torn from her. And the word murmured by the voice, what was it? She couldn't remember.

When she got up to have breakfast, her joints always ached. She couldn't understand why she felt so run-down. She had talked about it to Jordan, who had reminded her mother, very sweetly, that she was getting on. She was at last feeling her age. But Clarissa wouldn't have it. It had all started since she had moved here. And while the medical checkups she went through in her bathroom showed nothing abnormal, she was convinced her fatigue had something to do with the residence. She began to feel suspicious about the tap water; she stopped drinking it and ordered bottled mineral water through the weekly shopping drone. She also decided to stop taking the vitamin treatment Dr. Dewinter had prescribed. Facing the cameras, she pretended to swallow the pills, and ended up stuffing them into her pocket, then tossing them into the toilet bowl.

One morning, as she sat at her kitchen table rubbing her eyes, sleepy, her head still filled with haunting dreams, her ears still echoing from the murmur of the voice that whispered to her in the night, she heard the bizarre clicking noise that had startled Andy. She looked up. She thought she saw a trickle of powder sifting through the ceiling right into the mug of tea placed in front of her. At first, she believed she had been mistaken and it was just a trick of the light. But as she looked closely at her mug, a tiny coating of dust was quickly seeping into the liquid. She sat there, stunned. Had she imagined it? She got up, taking her time, and stared up at the light fixture above her head. It seemed perfectly normal. She spilled her tea into the sink, trying to act as naturally as possible. She was being watched. She rinsed the cup several times.

Thinking about the powder shadowed her all day long. What was that powder? Had it been poured into her tea every day? Was that why she felt tired, almost drugged? Why were "they" doing this? Whom could she talk to? She hadn't been able to work, to get on with her book. She acted like the cat, ill at ease, wary. She went to bed feeling uneasy. It seemed to her the cat looked even more nervous than usual.

Jordan had called her after dinner to organize Andy's next visit. She told her Aunt Serena's brooch was with a jewelry appraiser. She was convinced it wasn't worth much. She'd know in a week or so.

"You okay, Mums? Your voice sounds strange."

"I'm fine. A little tired. Nothing serious."

But her daughter wasn't giving up that easily.

"Hmmm, you've been saying that an awful lot lately. But I can tell there's something else. What's up?"

Clarissa ended up telling her about François. She admitted he had come there, had insisted upon speaking to her, and that she had gone down to meet him, to say it was all over. All this had stirred her up.

When she hung up, she noticed once again how her daughter had not asked her what François had done. But she knew Jordan's silence would not last. She knew Jordan would eventually harp on about this, and it wouldn't be because of an unhealthy curiosity, but, above all, impelled by the love she felt for her mother. Clarissa, aware of this, cherished her daughter's love, even if she felt at times that Jordan worried too much about her.

Sleep tumbled upon her like a leaden weight, for once. There had been no need to ask Mrs. Dalloway to display any videos, or for her to spy on her neighbors with her binoculars.

In the dead of the night, a strident blare drilled into her eardrums as the panic-stricken cat landed on her. A monstrously powerful alarm rang out, making the walls shudder. With distraught fingers, she tried to turn on the bedside lamp, but nothing happened. A blinking night-light feebly lit up the corridor with an unpleasant orange glow. Clarissa yelled out for Mrs. Dalloway to intervene, but the din was too loud.

A mechanical voice began to speak, repeating the same words over and over.

"STAY CALM. GET OUT NOW. FIRE ALARM. LEAVE PREMISES NOW. FIRE ALARM. GET OUT. WARNING. LEAVE NOW. LEAVE PREMISES NOW. WARNING."

She was only wearing her nightgown, and couldn't find her slippers or her dressing gown in the dimness. She had to leave; there was no time to locate them. From the armchair, she grabbed the sweater she had been wearing last evening, slipped it on with haste. There was a fire in the residence and she was on the top floor. She didn't have a minute to spare. Flustered, she seized the cat, and cried out in pain as he scratched her. She compressed him against her chest and flung herself into the dimly lit stairway. All the doors of the residence were opening up, and her neighbors emerged, disheveled and anxious. She followed the others down, while the cat twisted and turned, mewing frantically. The stairs seemed shadowy and endless. Suddenly, she heard Adelka's voice, felt her comforting palm against her elbow. She felt relief, even though she knew they still had more flights to go, that it wasn't over. In the huge hall, only the orange night-lights flickered. The alarm still howled and the voice went on giving orders.

"LEAVE THE RESIDENCE RIGHT AWAY. GET OUT. DANGER."

Head down, stumbling, Clarissa followed Adelka, clutching the squirming cat against her. The ground felt cold and damp to her bare feet. Outside, streetlamps shed a bright yellow light onto the small crowd. The residence loomed above them, clad in darkness. No flames, no smoke. The sirens were still howling. No one from the C.A.S.A. team was to be seen.

"Is there a fire, or what?" Adelka asked Clarissa. She noticed the cat and tickled him under his chin. "That's a very frightened kitty there, isn't it, now?" Chablis calmed down, but Clarissa could still feel his heart pumping under the soft fur.

"It's three in the morning!" mumbled a man in his thirties, standing next to them in a T-shirt and boxer shorts. "For fuck's sake, what's going on?"

He noticed Clarissa and Adelka looking at him and grinned apologetically. He held out his hand, introduced himself as Jim Perrier. Third floor.

"I'm wondering what C.A.S.A. has got up its sleeve," he said in a low voice.

"So there's no fire, you think?" asked Adelka, plucking a purring Chablis from Clarissa's arms. She obviously had a way with cats.

"I'm pretty sure there's no fire," said Jim.

"Unless it's a drill and they forgot to tell us," said Clarissa.

"That's what they'll probably come up with," said Jim.

"Maybe they wanted us all to get together and this was a clever way to do it," whispered Clarissa.

Jim looked at her and winked.

"You could very well be right," he whispered back.

Beyond the camaraderie of his wink, she felt perhaps she had found an ally, a person who had also become suspicious of what truly lay behind C.A.S.A. She wasn't the only one.

Clarissa looked around at her neighbors. She was familiar with anni's. Her mother was Italian, and her father French. She had grown up with both languages.

"That's funny," Clarissa remarked. "I'm bilingual, as well, French and English!"

"Are you torn between the two, as I am?"

"Precisely!"

"How amusing! Is there one you prefer over the other?"

"Nope. I can't choose. I'm attached to both."

Adelka's athletic figure was highlighted by a fetching blue dress.

"What would you like, red wine or white?"

"White, please."

While she prepared their drinks, Adelka asked if she'd seen their charming neighbor, Jim Perrier.

"No," said Clarissa carefully.

She had picked out the cameras. She was not going to reveal what Jim had told her. She still had not heard back from him. He must be busy. This had been going on for too long, she thought. But how could she contact him? She'd been back to Café Iris several times, at eight. He'd never turned up. She'd asked the waiters, and they hadn't seen him, either. But one of them had laughed, saying it wasn't surprising, as Jim regularly got plastered. Perhaps he'd gone off to a rehab? Clarissa had found it all puzzling.

Adelka handed her a wineglass.

"I rather fancy Jim. . . . Okay, he's a trifle young for me, but he's so hot in his underwear!"

Clarissa laughed with her, and they raised their glasses.

"After that alarm business, I bumped into him one evening, coming home. We went to a bar and chatted. He's a hard drinker! We had a great time. But he's dead set against C.A.S.A."

"Really?" asked Clarissa innocently. "Why?"

"Do you remember our talk, the night the alarm went off, when we were all outside?"

"More or less."

"You were convinced C.A.S.A. was spying on artists living in the residence, for God knows what reason. I said you both had too much imagination!"

"That's right! We write stories, he and I. Occupational hazard!"

"Jim is up in arms against Dewinter and her methods. He bombarded me with questions: Was I comfortable here? Did I sleep well? Did I ever hear a strange clicking sound? I told him I never had, that I slept like a log. What about you?"

"Me?"

"Are you getting used to it here? You told me even the cat was acting strange in your flat."

She had to be cautious. Pick the right words. Avoid triggering suspicion. She said, casually, that in the beginning, she'd found it hard to settle down in this new space. She'd only just left her husband, and felt miserable and overwrought. She slept better now. So did the cat. And as for the clicking sound, she never heard it again. All was well. It had just been a matter of time.

The fibs flowed, effortlessly.

"I'm so relieved!" exclaimed Adelka. "I was worried. I'm thrilled you've settled in at last. I love my life here. Living in the residence is like a dream come true. I feel safe here, and I work well. I really appreciate the C.A.S.A. team, their thoughtfulness, their expertise."

Clarissa forced her lips into a smile.

"As for Dr. Dewinter," Adelka went on, "what an extraordinary woman! She's remarkably intelligent, don't you find?"

"Remarkably." Clarissa nodded. "Tell me, you don't mind being filmed all the time?"

"Well, the bedroom camera can be switched to 'intimate mode.' Did you know that?"

"Actually, I didn't."

"I didn't, either! Ben told me. 'Intimate mode' can be turned on if you want to have sex or something." She giggled. "So the only thing missing for me in this ideal setting is a boyfriend!"

"Well, what about Jim? Did he remain impervious to your charms?"

"Utterly!"

They laughed together again.

"I even invited him here, would you believe it! I contacted him through the internal server, but he never answered."

"Was this recently?"

"A couple of days ago. I'm mortified! I must have been coming on too strong."

Adelka made a face.

"Perhaps he's on a business trip?" suggested Clarissa.

"Probably. Or he went to see his family? He mentioned his mother lived in Brussels."

Adelka had not had a serious relationship since she had broken up with her violent husband. She wanted children. More and more women were having them late, and on their own. Her mother had friends who had gotten pregnant at over sixty. It had become common. The modern medical world was astounding. But she didn't want to wait that long.

"I understand," said Clarissa as Adelka filled her glass up again. The white wine was making her deliciously tipsy.

"At what age did you become a mother?"

"Quite young. Twenty-seven or so."

A small silence. Then Clarissa added, "Two years before my daughter, Jordan, came into the world, I had a son. Stillborn. Forty-six years ago."

Adelka put her hand to her mouth.

"Oh! How terribly sad!"

"I can talk about it now, a little, but for many years, I simply couldn't."

"Did you see a therapist?"

"I did," said Clarissa, "but something else helped me. I didn't believe in it at first, but it changed my life."

"What was it?" asked Adelka, intrigued.

"Hypnosis."

"I don't know much about hypnosis, and have never tried it. Would you mind telling me some more?"

"Of course."

Clarissa told her how she'd gone to the first consultation dragging her feet, persuaded it was not going to work out. At that point, it had been twenty years or so since the baby's death, twenty years of not getting over it. Psychoanalysts, antidepressants, nothing had helped. Her first husband had ended up leaving her, powerless in the face of her enduring unhappiness. Her second husband, François, the one who was persona non grata, as Adelka recalled, had been convinced it could be the solution for her. She had to give it a go. Little by little, he'd managed to sway her. Clarissa said she'd try it out. She could no longer bear her situation. Things had to change, not only for her but for her entourage, especially her daughter. She presumed her daughter still bore the stigma of spending her childhood and adolescence with a melancholy mother burdened by sorrow. Jordan had never brought this up, but Clarissa thought it was the case. And it was probably why Jordan was still concerned about her mother, even today. She knew her daughter loved her, and how lucky she was. And then there was her granddaughter, the sunshine of her life.

"I think I caught a glimpse of you two together. A cute teen all dressed in black?"

"That's her! At the ripe old age of fourteen, Adriana is, I feel, the one person who understands me and knows me the best."

She went on with her story. Adelka had to picture her arriving at this Mrs. Delaporte's place. Clarissa had had no idea of what to expect. She'd found herself facing a brunette of her own age, slim and elegant, with large dark eyes. Elise Delaporte had asked her to take her place in an armchair positioned in the middle of a tastefully decorated living room. She asked her to close her eyes. Clarissa obeyed. In the beginning, the pleasant voice relaxed her, asking her to let go, to get rid of all the tensions in her body. Her neck, shoulders, chest, stomach, thighs, shins, and feet all mellowed; her rigidity melted. Clarissa allowed herself to be carried away—an agreeable sensation. If that was all there was to it . . . She could already see herself telling François it had been a sort of winding-down exercise. The voice acted upon her like a sedative. She felt her body yield, on the threshold of a peculiar torpor.

Even if Clarissa still heard her perfectly, Elise Delaporte seemed farther and farther away. It was as if Clarissa had departed elsewhere. She remained wholly conscious; she perceived the tang of Elise's lemony fragrance; she could hear the murmur of the traffic floating up to them, the footsteps of a neighbor overhead, but she felt as if she had stepped into a dark nook that seemed to deepen. At the far end of the niche, which had nothing alarming about it, and which she instinctively identified as a shelter, appeared a pale glow, a quivering stroke summoning her like a beacon, and she felt compelled to follow it. How long did this last? She hardly knew. She was hovering within a reassuring Milky Way created by Elise alone. She was on familiar territory. She had nothing to fear.

Clarissa stopped.

"Oh, please go on!" begged Adelka. "May I offer you more wine?"

"Why not?"

The wine slowed her down, giving her a languid pleasure she hadn't experienced in a long time. She took up her story. Elise Delaporte had asked her to describe a secret place that did her good, gave her peace. A real or an imaginary place. To answer her, it had been difficult for Clarissa to locate her own vocal cords. She felt she had forgotten how to speak, while being weightless, and when she finally managed to utter a few words, it seemed like her body and her voice were no longer one. The shrill, almost child-like tone sounded like a stranger's. After a moment's hesitation, she succeeded in describing a lake, and how its deepness pacified her. During that first session, they had concentrated on the lake's image.

Could she tell Adelka what had happened next, with all those cameras now filming and taping? The wine quelled her hesitancy. Adelka possessed the same upbeat vitality as Jordan. Why not open up to her? She discreetly pointed to the surveillance cameras, and the young woman understood, moving closer. Clarissa went on in a low whisper, while her head spun around and around. A couple of weeks later, during the second or the third session, something happened, something she had never been able to forget. Elise had asked her to describe what she saw at the bottom of that lake. Clarissa had seen herself diving into the greenish abyss, holding her breath, slowly going down deeper and deeper while the water became blurred and icy. She was freezing, shivering. She was afraid of no longer being able to breathe, not being able to get back up in time, and there, right at the bottom, buried in the mud lining the base of the lake, she had spotted a square object, a kind of box. A hideous fear had grabbed at her; she wanted to rise up to the surface, to open her mouth wide in order to breathe in oxygen, to escape from that box and whatever it contained.

But while the fluctuating white lace twirled on the inside of her eyelids, Elise's tranquil tone had soothed her. Elise said she must not be afraid of what that box enclosed; she must open it, take stock of it. She had to face it. Clarissa saw herself seizing the box, wrangling to unbolt it in spite of the rusty lock. The top swung open, and inside was a baby. Her son. Her son exactly as she had beheld him after birth, his downy hair, his miniature face, his waxen skin. There, at the bottom of the lake, she clasped her son's body between her hands. She had nearly screamed, given away to her panic, pain, and anguish; she had nearly drowned in it all, surrendered to the lake's vortexes, but Elise's voice had come to guide her, and she had held on with all her might to the strength of that very voice. Clarissa described everything she saw and felt, and Elise was there with her, by her side, under the water, her hair mingling with Clarissa's own. She was telling her to let the baby go, not to put it back in the box, to hug it one last time, to say good-bye. Clarissa had embraced her son, kissing the little forehead, and she had opened up her hands; her son's body had been set free, gliding up to the surface, and she had followed it with her eyes until it became a tiny white spot.

Tears had spurted, fountainlike, trickling along her cheeks, her neck, moistening her chest. The sorrow was slipping away, gradually, teardrop after teardrop, sob after sob, and she felt it departing at last. When Elise had asked her to open her eyes, slowly, after counting to five, Clarissa felt a physical exhaustion she had rarely known, but beyond that tiredness, she found she had to learn how to welcome a novel peace lodged profoundly within her. She knew—she could tell—the pain had gone. She could now get on with her life. The wound was still there, and it would always be, but Clarissa now knew how to live with it, and how to tame it. She had seen Elise Delaporte only a couple of times after that. She hadn't needed any more sessions.

Adelka's dark eyes had gone liquid. She took Clarissa's hand, squeezed it. Speaking in a low tone, she thanked her for sharing such a touching memory. Clarissa said the path to writing had opened up for her shortly after. Freed from her grief, she'd felt the need to explore what she'd experienced in Romain Gary's and Virginia Woolf's wake, writers devoted to places, through their writing, their creativeness, but also because they'd chosen to die at home, at the heart of their intimate territories. She'd decided to start with her own emotions, her personal path, but this was set to become a novel, not her story. Adelka said she was engrossed by *Topography of Intimacy*. It wasn't at all the type of book she usually read, but she was enjoying it. It was startling, strange, and unexpected. Clarissa approved of her forthrightness. This young woman had nothing of a hypocrite about her. She appreciated that.

The rest of the evening went smoothly. They talked without worrying about the cameras. Adelka opened another bottle of wine, proffered cheese, bread, and olives. She discussed her work, how she recruited her models, where she chose to show her paintings. Clarissa had too much to drink. She wasn't used to it. Trying not to lurch, she left late, at midnight, telling Adelka she didn't need to be seen up to the eighth floor. What an idiot, getting sloshed at her age! It was almost funny. Almost. While she waited for the elevator, lacking the courage to go up by foot, she recalled Jim Perrier lived just below, on the third floor. Holding on to the banister as best as she could, she went down. Initials J.P. on the doorbell. She rang. It was probably too late, she knew. Too bad. No response. She waited. Where the hell was he? She tried once more. No answer. This was becoming both alarming and incomprehensible.

The residence cloaked her with oppressing silence. She stood within the cushy stairwell, the walls coated in sophisticated hues, and she viewed it all with abhorrence. She was fed up with being spied on. She had fled François and his repugnant secret, to find shelter here. She thought she had succeeded.

But the C.A.S.A. residence was no haven.

She could not sleep. She was hoping the wine might help her drop off, but the opposite happened. Her eyes remained wide open. She tried herbal tea, a shower, watching her neighbors; nothing worked. Lying on her bed, Chablis at her side, she asked Mrs. Dalloway to show her soothing videos of oceans and lakes. She sank into a semisomnolent state, one she knew only too well since she'd moved in and that she loathed, with the frustrating impression that she could no longer distinguish reality from her dreams. Was she asleep? Awake? She couldn't tell. The wine had confused the issue. That word was coming back again and again, the same word, like an unrelenting wave bashing into her ears.

That word filling up the entire space, seeping into her skull; she must figure out what it was. In the dimness, while the lake's surface crinkled the ceiling, she forced herself to regain consciousness. *Listen. Concentrate. Listen.* Night after night, she heard that voice, that word. *One final effort. Now.*

That voice. How was it possible? Yet it seemed to be that voice, light as the breeze, as the rustle of leaves, or the murmur of the turning tide. Elise's voice? Clarissa struggled to remain calm, staring into the dark. No panicking. She had to keep it all in, to reveal nothing. Now, she could only make out silence, but had it really been Elise speaking to her, in the deepest hour, every night? And that word over and over, striking right at her heart?

Her son's name. Her baby. The name Toby and she had chosen with such care, such love. The name written on the simple tombstone at Montparnasse Cemetery, where their son was laid to rest, and where she never went, because the pain, as soon as she drew near, became unbearable.

Had she dreamed it? Had she craved hearing that name so badly, she'd let it bloom within her own ear? No, of course not! She hadn't dreamed a thing!

Fury swept over her, a nameless violence scorching the pit of her stomach. She leaped out of bed, howling with rage, brandishing her fist. How dared "they"? How could "they" do this? Manipulate her this way? Was that why she'd had to endure that tedious setting-up process? So that her past would come back to haunt her? What for? Now she could see why her nights were brief, bedecked with tears, preventing her from getting ahead, from writing her book.

"What the hell are you up to?" she spat out, glaring at one of the cameras. "And you there, hiding behind your screens, snooping on me, what are you waiting for? For me to go bonkers, is that it? Is that your intention? My going off the deep end? So that's C.A.S.A. protocol, is it? Well done!"

Mrs. Dalloway made herself heard, unflappable.

"I'm sorry, Clarissa, I don't understand what you are trying to tell me. Please rephrase."

"Shut up!" shouted Clarissa, beside herself with wrath. "Just shut the fuck up!"

"I'm sorry, Clarissa. What, exactly, is the problem?"

"Be quiet! Can you understand that? Here it is one more time: Stop talking to me!"

"I'm sorry, I don't understand your demand."

Silence. Clarissa got a grip on herself.

"Mrs. Dalloway," she hissed.

"Yes, Clarissa?"

"I don't want to hear you."

"Fine, Clarissa. You can deactivate voice mode. You only have to say it."

"Mrs. Dalloway, deactivate voice mode."

An icon glowed on the nearby wall, confirming her order had been taken into account.

"Deactivate all cameras."

A sentence showed up. *It is impossible to deactivate the cameras.*

"Go to hell! Deactivate everything."

It is impossible to deactivate everything.

Clarissa unleashed a volley of abuse worthy of her father's— the kind that used to cause her mother such displeasure. It was exhilarating. She felt lighter, less tense. She even grinned. Chablis came purring against her shins. She took him into the living room, her nose buried in the soft fur.

"What would I do without you, cat?"

She lay down on the sofa with him. Dawn was about to break, lighting up the rooftops with a pink touch. Tiredness took over, and she dozed on and off. A few hours later, when she got up, still exhausted, with a painful back, it was broad daylight. It was strange and liberating not to hear Mrs. Dalloway greeting her, like she used to every morning. The weather forecast, the main headlines, and her agenda silently appeared on the mural panels in large fonts, so her shortsighted eyes could read without glasses. Andy was coming later on today, to spend the night.

"Please send an internal message to Adelka Miki."

Go ahead.

"Thank you for a lovely evening. I had a great time with you. I overdid it with the white wine, and getting up this morning was ghastly! But I have no regrets. See you soon! Clarissa."

I've sent it.

"Please send an internal message to Jim Perrier."

Go ahead.

"Hi Jim! Hope you're well. I thought of a producer who might be interested in adapting my first novel for TV. I'd be happy to discuss this with you. All best, Clarissa."

Message rejected by server.

Clarissa read the sentence a couple of times, perplexed.

"Why is the message rejected? I don't understand."

There is no Jim Perrier in the residence.

"What? That's impossible; he lives on the third floor. There must be a mistake. Try again."

The name Jim Perrier is not recognized by C.A.S.A. protocol. Message rejected by server.

Clarissa remained silent. She must not reveal her distress; she must take it in stride. For a couple of minutes, she forced herself to calm down. When she felt less strained, she went into the bathroom to undergo the medical tests. Using a loud, contemptuous tone, she said, "Are you eventually going to notice how tired I am?

And perhaps a surprisingly high alcohol level? What do you do with all those results? Oh, I'm not expecting any answers!"

In the mirror, she glimpsed her crumpled features, her lackluster hair, her dry skin. The C.A.S.A. effect? Did the other artists feel this way, as well? Adelka, on the contrary, appeared to be blossoming.

Jim Perrier. His name haunted her all day. Had he made a discovery concerning the powder that could have led to his eviction? Was he in danger? He had warned her that mobile devices and computers were under surveillance. How could she reach him? She didn't dare make any online searches in order to try to locate him. But she also knew he had a drinking problem, which Adelka had noticed, as well as the waiters at Café Iris. She wondered if she could go on trusting him.

At the end of the day, she decided to wait for Andy outside the residence, near the Tower Memorial. They could speak without being listened to. The young girl was surprised to see her grandmother waiting for her on a bench, and even more so when she saw her haggard face.

"It's no big deal," mumbled Clarissa. "Another lousy night. I have lots to tell you. Inside, we can't talk. Sit down and listen to me."

She related the powder incident, and Jim Perrier's vanishing act. She was concerned. Something was going on in that damned residence, and she couldn't figure out what. She was convinced her sleep was being tampered with. Apart from Andy, Jim was the only person she could bring this up with. And now he was gone. Andy listened attentively. Clarissa was fearfully expecting her granddaughter to tell her she was getting the wrong ideas. But Andy began to talk in a calm and thoughtful manner.

"Quit putting on that scared expression, Mums. I've been on your side since the beginning. And I have stuff to say that corroborates your point of view. I got in touch with the University of East

Anglia, attended by our dear Mia White. They never responded to my email, so I phoned them. I passed myself off as a silly friend with a French accent who was trying to get hold of her. I must be kind of talented, because they fell for it. Guess what? Mia White got her diploma last year. She's no longer a student. Odd, no? It gave me the wildest ideas! What if that girl is here to spy on you? What if she's been working for C.A.S.A. all along?"

Clarissa gazed at her granddaughter. She seemed so mature, so confident.

"So that would explain why I thought I saw her downstairs the night the alarm went off."

"You did? My guess is that she sleeps here and watches you nonstop. You're her full-time job."

"What do these people want, Andy?"

Andy slipped an arm around Clarissa's shoulder.

"No hassle, Mums. We're going to find out."

"But how? They see everything I do."

"I know. We have to start thinking hard. There must be something all these artists have in common. That's what they're after. Dr. Dethingy, you know she's an AI hotshot. I've been looking her up."

"Yes, Jim did, as well."

"My guess is that she went rogue. Impossible to find out what she's been up to. In your day, people went on the dark web to hunt for that sort of stuff, but now, that's so mainstream and what you find there has nothing juicy about it. Digging deep into the blacker web might bring answers about the doctor's activities, but that's tricky. I'd need help. I could ask around. I have a friend whose brother is one of those new detectives, or a spy, if you prefer. His thing is politics. He knows how to drag up all the stuff people don't ever want anyone to find. He earns millions."

"How do you know all this, Andy?"

"Everyone knows, Mums. I didn't start it."

"I'm all at sea, over here."

"I know, and that's normal. Don't worry, I'm not going to do anything foolish. We have two simple missions here. One, what happened to your pal Jim? Two, what is behind C.A.S.A.? Meanwhile, when we get to your place, we act normal. As usual, okay? And if we need to talk, we write on bits of paper."

"You're brilliant, Andy."

"Not at all, Mums, just trying to help out. Do you a have a list of all the artists who live in the residence?"

"Yes, at home. Why?"

"I'd like to take a look at it. Perhaps it's all in that list."

"What do you mean?"

"You're all artists, so you have that in common. But apart from your professions, there must be something else about you that C.A.S.A. finds interesting."

Clarissa glanced around her. The sun, shining bright and strong, was hurting her eyes. Lately, the weather had been persistently hot and sunny, even if summer was not yet here. It had rained only a couple of times, and when it had, it had poured down with fierce devastation.

"Mummy says a new heat wave is lined up for next week."

"Not another one!"

Jordan was given all climatic data in advance, due to her job.

"Yep, and she says this one will be a scorcher. It's going to set a new record, going up to forty-eight degrees Celsius."

Clarissa sighed.

"Let's go home, Mums. You look tired. Let me take care of you."

"You're such a sweetie. Hey, missy, you're going to love this. I managed to get Mrs. Dalloway to shut up. I only had to turn voice mode off. Now everything she says is written on the wall. That's it. And it's bliss."

They were on their way, arms linked. Clarissa walked at a slow pace, with difficulty. She'd felt old ever since this morning. A wreck. Once they got home, she went to fetch the neighbor list. Andy looked at it for a while. Then she folded it and put it in her pocket. She helped her grandmother prepare her favorite dinner. They called Toby. The conversation was spontaneous and amusing. Just before they sat down to eat, Andy made a face.

"Oh, shucks! No more salt, right?" she said.

While her back was turned to the camera, she winked in Clarissa's direction.

"I'll get some from your neighbors."

A beaming smile, a cup grabbed from the shelf, and out she rushed. Clarissa put a lid on the soup and kept the potatoes in the oven. She turned on the news, trying to act normal. An unparalleled heat wave was indeed forecast for next week, about to descend upon Paris and its outskirts. About twenty minutes later, Andy returned with a small smile and the cup filled with salt. She devoured her dinner with her usual appetite and spoke little during the meal. Clarissa waited. She suspected her granddaughter was onto something. She longed to ask questions, but abstained. They put the dishes away while Andy whistled.

"How about a movie, Mums?"

"With pleasure. Which one?"

"Something vintage. You choose!"

"Ever heard of *Barry Lyndon*?"

"Rings a bell. Any good?"

Clarissa smiled.

"I saw it for the first time when I was your age."

"You liked it?"

"More than liked it."

"Okay. Let's go for it."

"Stanley Kubrick is my favorite filmmaker."

"That, I knew! Mummy's told me often enough!"

They settled down in the living room, with the cat on Andy's lap. Clarissa asked Mrs. Dalloway to find the movie *Barry Lyndon* and play it.

"How fabulous it is to no longer hear that Dalloway voice. Good job, Mums."

Then Andy whispered in Clarissa's ear, asking her to turn the sound up high.

Clarissa obeyed. The volume was so loud that Clarissa's eardrums ached. Andy played with a wisp of her own hair, which she kept placing in front of her lips. She murmured, "Can you hear me, Mums? Look straight ahead. Stick something on your mouth—your mug, for example."

"Roger that."

"Wow! That guy is so hot!" yelled Andy. "Who is he?"

"Ryan O'Neal."

"Is he still around?"

"He's your great-grandpa's age."

"You think he has a great-grandson?"

Andy was swept away by the magnificent images, by Handel's haunting sarabande.

The whispering took up again.

"I'm going to go to the loo. No cameras in there, right? I'll call out, saying there's no more toilet paper. You'll fetch some and bring it to me. Okay?"

Clarissa nodded, unnoticeably.

A couple of minutes later, her granddaughter was heard.

"Hey, Mums! End of loo paper!"

"Coming, miss."

She got up, cursing at the backache that seemed to be here to stay. She went into her bathroom, fetched the tissue roll from her cupboard. Andy let her in the toilet room and closed the door behind her.

"I got it. Your neighbors."

"What? Tell me!"

"Don't talk so loudly. I didn't see all of them; some weren't at home. But I did notice they're not all purely French."

"You sound like our awful president when you say that."

"Listen. Listen carefully. They're like you. Bicultural."

She took the paper out of her pocket and unfolded it.

"Arlen, from Montreal. Bell, from Australia. Engeler, not there. Fromet, supergluey, poured her heart out. She has an English mum. Holzmann, from Germany. Azoulay, Morocco. Olsen and Miki, not home."

"Adelka Miki's mother is Italian."

"Aha. See? And your buddy Perrier?"

"Belgian mother. I believe he speaks Flemish."

"Pomeroy, charming, from San Francisco. Rachewski, from Saint Petersburg. Van Druten, Amsterdam. Zajak, not home."

"What's your point, missy?"

It was beginning to get warm in the tiny space.

"You're all bilingual. You all speak two languages fluently."

Clarissa's pulse quickened.

"Andy! Mia White!"

"Yes, what about her?"

"Franco-British, like me."

Andy waved the paper around theatrically.

"The mind reels. What if C.A.S.A. was studying the lot of you because you have hybrid brains, as you like to call it? And what if dear bilingual Mia White was the project leader on all this?"

The cat was anxiously waiting for them. They returned to the screen, not speaking to each other. Clarissa found she could no longer concentrate on the movie. She kept thinking back to the numerous questions Mia White had asked her about bilingualism, trying to remember her own answers.

Andy was scribbling something on a bit of paper. She handed it over to her.

On the third floor, door on the left was ajar. Jim Perrier's place. Wasn't able to see inside. I rang; no one answered.

Clarissa continued to stare at the screen, transfixed. Andy mumbled, "We need to go check this out. Later. When everyone's off in the land of nod."

The entire building was still. Not a single noise to be heard. The night-lights were switched on, casting a pallid glimmer into the depths of the stairwell. Clarissa and Andy waited until two in the morning. They watched another movie, or pretended to, more or less dropping off in front of it; then they turned off all the lights, faked going to bed, lying down in the dark, fully clothed. Clarissa activated "intimate mode." They quietly slipped out of the flat.

Jim Perrier's door was ajar. It only needed to be pushed in order to open wide. Inside, a patch of darkness. Andy turned on her mobile's flashlight. Clarissa pondered if this was a good idea. What would they ever do, or say, if they were found here? But Andy was already striding ahead, fearless. What an amazing little person. But then she thought of Jordan. Her daughter would be furious, no doubt.

"Come on!" murmured Andy. "There's no one here."

The space had been entirely stripped. Andy moved the flashlight over the walls and floors. Everything was empty, as if no one had ever lived here. Clarissa thought of Jim Perrier, in his underwear, the night the alarm went off. His pleasant cologne. Where was he now?

"Watch out for those cameras," whispered Clarissa. "'They' will detect us soon enough."

"In my opinion, nothing's on," said Andy. "The virtual assistant is off, as well. We have nothing to be afraid of. They're not going to film a vacant apartment."

They padded into the kitchen, then the bathroom.

"What if Jim was expelled by C.A.S.A.," said Andy, "because he knew too much?"

"Or maybe because of his drinking problem?"

"Whatever it was, C.A.S.A. didn't approve."

"Maybe he's the one who took off—"

"Shh!" commanded Andy, interrupting her. "There's someone there, just outside."

Clarissa was petrified. Her stomach churned uncomfortably. Who could it be, out there? Ben? Dr. Dewinter? She'd have to think up some sort of excuse to explain what they were doing here. Panic took over.

"Get into that wardrobe over there, Mums. Let me take charge. I know what to do."

"But . . ."

"Do what I say. I can handle this. Trust me."

Clarissa dashed into the hiding place, taking care to leave the door slightly open. From there, she could glimpse the entrance, where Andy had lain down on the floor, as if she were asleep. What on earth was she doing?

The noise Andy had picked up was now making its way to her own ears: an odd hissing sound. Andy was still flat out, motionless. Clarissa held her breath. The presence materialized, crossed the threshold. The form she beheld had nothing human about it; it was a large steel wheel, moving forward with metallic clicks. The circle halted when it came to Andy, and then, under Clarissa's agitated and incredulous gaze, it lengthened out, modifying itself, changing its shape. She saw a long iron silhouette slowly unfold, taking its time, unfurling upward as it grazed the ceiling. Clarissa had never seen one in true life before, but she knew what it was. And Jim had mentioned it. A Bardi. One of the most elaborate and redoubtable guard robots ever, overpriced and efficient. At the end of each extremity, it bore a set of electrocuting pincers. Two round gleaming LED lights acted as its eyes. The Bardi had something of a Giacometti statue about it, with its long, lean, and elegant lines, and seemed harmless, but Clarissa had read enough about them to know what a Bardi was capable of. How could she get Andy out of this? She thought of Jordan. Ivan.

The Bardi had located Andy's body on the floor. It came onward with that menacing skid that compressed Clarissa's heart. The red beam flickered over Andy, who pretended to awaken.

"Get up."

A mechanical, androgynous voice.

Andy rose, unperturbed. How was she able to remain so calm? Clarissa also knew the robots were equipped with facial recognition. The red spotlights lit up Andy's face and then locked onto her eyes.

"The individual is a minor recognized by C.A.S.A. protocol. Adriana Garnier. Explain the reason of your presence on these premises."

Adriana did not lose countenance. She lifted her chin to be able to stare back at the robot. It had bent over in order to examine her more closely, and Clarissa could make out the details of the startling metallic features, and the two small horns planted on each side of its head, giving it an animal-like aspect.

"I'm the granddaughter of Clarissa Katsef, the writer on the eighth floor. I was supposed to meet the person who lives here. But Jim never turned up. I fell asleep waiting for him."

The silent robot appeared to ingest the information.

"The door was open," Andy went on smoothly. "So I just came in."

"Your mobile."

The iron pincer made its way toward Andy, opening up to form a flat surface.

"I don't mind showing it to you, but you won't find traces of any of our texts. I erased them all."

"Why?"

Andy shrugged.

"I don't want my parents breathing down my neck. They don't know about my relationship with Jim."

"Hand over your mobile."

Andy obeyed. She placed the phone in the little tray. A throbbing noise was heard.

"Thank you. You may take it back. Go up to your grandmother's place and do not come back here."

Andy seemed to hesitate; then she said, "Where is Jim Perrier, please?"

"There is no Jim Perrier here."

"But where is he? Why did he disappear? Why is his apartment empty?"

"Go back upstairs."

"I'd like to know what happened to Jim!"

"Do not argue with me."

The robot slid forward and touched Adriana's arm with its right pincer. The snapping sound of an electric shock was heard.

"What the fuck?" bawled the young girl. "I've done nothing wrong!"

"Go upstairs. Get out of here."

"Okay! I got the message! I'm leaving!"

The robot shoved Andy toward the entry, claws brandished like weapons. Clarissa heard the door bang shut. She waited, frightened, her chest feeling tight. She'd let a few minutes slip by; then she'd rush upstairs to join Andy.

Jim Perrier's vacant flat seemed dark all of a sudden. The only thing she could hear was her slightly ragged breath. Apprehension pulsed through her once more. What had she done, following Andy? She longed to be back home, all snug, with Andy and the cat. A mug of herbal tea and off to bed. If Jim Perrier could see her now, cowering with fear in his empty wardrobe. She could picture his grin.

A faint hissing sound was heard, and her heart froze. She

pricked up her ears. There it was again. She hadn't gotten it wrong. The Bardi had remained inside. It hadn't left. It must have understood there was a presence in the apartment. It was coming back for her, like a bloodhound. Horrified, Clarissa crawled to the back of the wardrobe.

The robot slid along, unhurried, with the slight squeak she had learned to fear, while its face swung methodically from left to right. She knew it was equipped with sensors capable of picking out body heat. From her hiding place, she could make out the reddish glow of its two LEDs piercing the gloom. It was coming closer, slowly but surely, and it was going to find her. She could imagine the steel claws clamping onto her arm. She felt like she was going to pass out.

A series of loud reiterated knocks on the door made her jump. The robot stopped moving, only a few feet away from her. It swiveled back toward the entrance. Clarissa heard Andy's shout.

"I want to know where Jim Perrier is! I want to know where my friend is!"

"Jim Perrier no longer lives here. Go home. Immediately."

"But he told me to meet him here! Something is going on!"

"If you don't leave, you'll have to come with me."

"I'm a minor!" wailed Andy. "You can't just take me with you, and besides, I've done nothing wrong."

"Leave."

"If I go upstairs, will you leave, as well?" asked Andy.

Clarissa was amazed by her granddaughter's audacity.

"Yes, I will depart if you go upstairs," came the robotic tone.

"Watch me, Mr. Bardi! I'm going up! Look! See?"

Andy's voice became fainter.

Clarissa waited, her stomach still painful, her breath short. She couldn't bear it if the Bardi came back. She peered out from behind the crack of the wardrobe door. The robot had stopped talking; it appeared frozen. Then, suddenly, it twisted down with an unexpectedly graceful swoop, coiled itself up, and took on the circle aspect it had when it arrived. Clarissa heard it roll down the steps.

A couple of minutes later, Andy called out.

"Mums! Get out of there! Hurry!"

Clarissa leaped out, not knowing where she was going, hands held out, and ended her wild rush, gasping for breath in Andy's arms. The front door on the right of the landing opened, and an elegant man in his sixties appeared, wearing a blue dressing gown. He glanced at them cautiously.

"Is everything all right? I heard some noise."

He had an American accent, blue eyes. Andy smiled at him reassuringly and answered him in English. They were very sorry; it was so late! She'd seen him earlier on; she'd come to ask for salt. Sean Pomeroy, right? From San Francisco. Clarissa introduced herself in turn, explained they were looking for his neighbor, Jim Perrier. Sean Pomeroy replied that he hadn't seen him for a while. Perhaps he'd moved. Then he added, with a mischievous smile, "A rather raucous young man."

"Oh?" said Clarissa.

"Let's say he often came home drunk and got the doors mixed up."

They said good night. Going up in the elevator, Clarissa told herself this amiable gentleman must have thought they were mad. She couldn't get over what they had just done. The risk of it all! The danger! But she couldn't bring herself to scold Adriana. Her granddaughter looked back at her with quiet triumph in her eyes.

When they got to the eighth floor, Clarissa asked her to make sure there was no Bardi lurking around. Andy checked.

"No Bardi, Mums. Just a poor cat mewing behind the door."

Clarissa descended into a troubled slumber, with the memory of the Bardi's red eyes chasing her. She awoke at dawn, and lay there, listening to Andy breathing. She waited until the young girl opened her eyes and smiled at her. What a marvelous thing, Adriana's smile.

"I had such weird dreams, Mums."

"House specialty, I'd say!"

Andy yawned and stretched her limbs.

"You were talking in your sleep, Mums. You kept repeating the same word over and over in a soft little voice."

Clarissa stiffened.

"What word?"

"A name."

"Which name?"

"Glenn."

Clarissa shut her eyes. She felt exhaustion take over and govern her. She wanted to curl up and never get out of bed; in the pit of her stomach, she felt a load where she had carried her dead child. She couldn't believe she had been saying his name out loud during her sleep.

"Mums. You don't have to explain."

Andy's small hand found her own.

"I know who Glenn is. Mummy told me a long time ago she had an older brother who died at birth. Your son. I've never talked about it with you. I was waiting. Take your time. If we don't talk now, it will be at another moment."

Then Andy whispered resolutely, "I don't know what the hell they want, or what they're doing, and maybe we will never find out. But I do know one thing. You have to get out of here, Mums. Pronto."

NOTEBOOK

Afterward, I had to write it all down. Describe it. I had to get it out of my system. The only way to do that was to create a distance. To protect myself.

The door, facing me. The key, in my hand. One final qualm. Turn around, leave, stay in the dark? Open up, discover it all? The choice appeared easy, in the beginning. But it became infernal as I lingered on the doorstep.

Door opening. No squeak. I slipped in easily. I had waited a long while, nearly an hour. I had rung the bell. Nobody had answered. The door was double-locked.

A small entrance. An overpowering, brash tone of purple. I was startled. I knew François preferred the elegant discretion of taupe, russet, dark blue, silver.

Another door. I breathed in whorls of potent and heavy feminine perfume. It was familiar. The one I had sniffed on my husband's jackets and shirts. Sickeningly sweet, like cotton candy.

The place felt stuffy, as if it wasn't ventilated often.

A single room, not large. Blinds lowered. Not much light. Night had fallen and it was hard to make anything out. Not a lot of furniture, apart from a huge four-poster bed that took center stage. It obscenely dominated all the rest. Purple, everywhere. Walls, fitted carpet, net curtains around the bed.

François was waiting for me at our friends' place for dinner. He had already sent several texts, wondering what I was doing, why I was late. I hadn't answered.

I had time, after all. But what if she came home? I hadn't thought about that. All of a sudden, I felt nervous. The perfume was making me uncomfortable.

Near the window, on a pedestal table, there was a framed photograph. I drew closer. It was her. Her, with him. They were hugging, on that dreadful gigantic bed.

She had curly blond hair. She was young, younger than Jordan. Thirty years old, give or take. A smooth, angelic face. The pink skin of a piglet. A beatific smile. Emotionless eyes. A plump body. She was wearing a negligée; he was bare-chested.

My eyes were beginning to get used to the penumbra. On the chest of drawers, photo albums. *Be careful. Watch out. Do you really want to look at those? Do you really want to see them? You already know everything there is to know. You know your husband is cheating on you with this young woman. You know they meet here, a couple of times a week. You should get the hell out of here. Now. Why torture yourself? Why look at those blasted albums?*

It was impossible to turn back. I looked at them all.

Romantic snacks, cocktails, champagne, birthday cakes, always here, in this vile purple chamber. My husband, soppy-eyed and smitten. Her affected smirk, her golden curls. He wore dark jackets and a tie; she, low-cut tunics. In one of the photos, she was sitting on his knees, wearing an evening dress. He was avidly suckling her breast.

Under the albums, I found a tablet, a smaller model. *Don't look. Resist. Put it down. Get out. Clear off.*

Too late. Twenty videos or so. It was so easy to press on the icons.

My heart had started to beat with a slow, devouring anger. Videos of them on the bed. Close-ups. Kisses. Tongues and genitals. Her vulva was entirely hairless. Her on top of him. Him on her. Him inside her. Him in her mouth, in between her bosoms, in between her buttocks. I watched it all. The slow, then frenzied to-and-fro. My hands trembled. It was appalling.

A mad urge to smash everything up. Wreak havoc. Decimate the place. Reduce it all to smithereens. But it didn't last. I was a sitting duck for grief and despondency. In that sordid room, I stood there, helpless and drained.

I went to check out the rest of the flat, switching on the lights. A tiny kitchen. Nothing in the refrigerator apart from champagne. Two glasses by the sink. Farther on, the bathroom. No lipstick, mascara, powder. Surprising, considering how made up she was in the videos. No beauty products. Just her perfume, on the shelf above the basin. They even shared a toothbrush. A stick of deodorant, for men. One large purple towel. In the shower, an item that looked like a long bottle brush for cleaning flasks, and a pear-shaped object made of black rubber.

Back in the bedroom, I drew closer to the four-poster, as if to behold it one last time, before I left for good. The mauve net curtains were drawn. On the single night table, a vintage Polaroid camera, and some lubricant gel.

I drew the voile curtain. I nearly screamed.

There was a figure, on the mattress. A woman, lying there on her side, her back to me, her long blond locks spread over the pillow.

8

HEAT WAVE

*Moments like this are buds on the tree of life. Flowers of
darkness they are . . .*

Virginia Woolf, *Mrs. Dalloway,* 1925

Instead of screaming, I write books.

Romain Gary, *Promise at Dawn,* 1960

IN THE PAST ten years, Paris had endured a string of heat
waves, but the one drawing closer, heralded by uncertainties,
concerns, speculations, and confusion of all kinds, was set to
be record-breaking. It was pronounced devastating, although it
was predicted to last forty-eight hours at the most. The president
had gone so far as to impose a nonworking day. Her minister for
health exhorted Parisians to remain at home. For those in need,
air-conditioned spaces were made available; bottled water was to
be delivered by drones at specific areas, and all emergency de-
partments were fully mobilized and on the alert. Trains were not
operating, because heat might distort railway tracks. Only a few
planes were allowed to take off. Public transport services were
reduced to the minimum. The latest heat wave, which came close
to forty-five degrees Celsius, was already an unpleasant memory,
but this one would be much worse. Irked, Clarissa listened to the

news. Why such doom-mongering? For the past day, the impending hot spell was described only in the most fear-provoking terms.

The residence was fully equipped with state-of-the-art air-conditioning, and for that, Clarissa was thankful. She had suggested Jordan and her little family come and stay during the hottest hours, but her daughter had declined. Jordan had some portable units that would do. They'd pull through. Why had Clarissa picked out a small shadow in Jordan's tone? Was she imagining things, or was Jordan resentful about something?

Fed up with the alarmist headlines, Clarissa turned off the newscast. Close the shutters, stay inside, drink enough water. Yes, she knew all that. Like thousands of Parisians, she endured both those commands and torrid temperatures several times a year. This morning, her father sent a message that made her laugh. From all his ninety-eight years of age, he reminded her that senior citizens, like herself, should be most vigilant during a heat wave. The last one had spelled carnage, did she recall? Fortunately, London was going to stay cool. Signed "Super Senior Citizen," her dad.

A little ping was heard. Mrs. Dalloway had something to say. Her words showed up on the wall for Clarissa to read.

FYI, mail has just been delivered. There's a letter for you. Handwritten. No return address.

Postal mail had become uncommon. Paper was no longer used for bills, love letters, or even condolences. People had stopped writing over the years; they sent text messages or emails. Clarissa was curious as to who had written her a letter the old-fashioned way. She went down to fetch it. She didn't see anyone. Had the artists all retreated to their homes in fear of the heat wave? She instantly recognized François's handwriting on the envelope. She didn't open it. When she got back upstairs, she slipped the letter into her handbag. Should she read it now? Courage failed her. She'd do it another day.

Her book was coming along slowly. Too slowly. She hid from surveillance to write in both her notebooks, the English one and the French one, but her heart was no longer in it. Leaving here had become her new fixation. Getting out of C.A.S.A. It ate up all the rest. She had signed a contract and a lease. She was going to have to check all that out again. And above all, wherever could she go? That unanswerable question preoccupied her.

The sky turned livid as the day progressed. She had never seen such a color. The sun beat down through the skylight, which she had not been able to black out. She entrenched herself in her bedroom, where the shutters could be closed. In the dimness, she felt safer. Chablis dozed. Clarissa thought about the multitude of air conditioners frantically struggling against irrational temperatures while spewing out hot air. She found the waiting unbearable. She received texts from friends making sure she was sheltered, looking after herself. She answered back reassuringly, heartened by the small tokens of affection.

The hours crawled by with extreme slowness. Everything felt sluggish. Andy called to see how her grandmother was doing. It wasn't too awful at theirs. But she wasn't looking forward to nighttime. Clarissa reminded her that she had suggested the family come over, and that Jordan had refused. Incomprehensible, according to Andy.

Clarissa found it impossible to read or write. She felt jittery, worried sick. She wasn't anxious for her own sake; she felt frightened for the city. Paris had never been through such high temperatures. She wondered if infrastructures were going to make it. She answered a call from Toby, watching over her, even from far away. She switched the TV on again, without the sound, gazed at the ghost-town streets of a deserted capital. Not a single car, not one pedestrian. All shops were closed. Only drones could be seen making their rounds, like huge insects hovering over empty boulevards. She could hear their rumble through the double glazing. She had always loathed that noise.

She unfastened a windowpane at four o'clock in the afternoon, just to see. The blistering air was a smack in the face, similar to opening an oven. Forty-five degrees Celsius in the shade. She was aware the digits were going to rise even higher. She felt protected in her cool home, but the escalating warmth, like the relentless loom of a calamity, shook her up. The news channels kept harking back to the death of the bees and its consequences, and showing the same perpetual images of climate disruption. The lifeless streets of Paris appeared to be the main focus of the media worldwide. Disheartened by the morose broadcasts, Clarissa asked Mrs. Dalloway to show the movie *Modern Times*.

She must have fallen asleep when Chaplin was being swallowed whole by the factory gearwheels, because when she opened her eyes, night had fallen. Her mouth felt furry; her head ached. When she rose, dizziness forced her down again. The cat lay listless in a corner. She hobbled to the kitchen. She couldn't find any bottles of mineral water in the refrigerator. Yet she was certain she had stocked up on them. She couldn't understand why they were nowhere to be seen. The throbbing of her head worsened; she felt like retching. She had to grip the furniture in order not to fall. Never in her entire life had she been so thirsty. Her entire body seemed parched. She began to shudder. There was no other choice than to drink from the tap, that water filtered by the residence, of which she was suspicious. The liquid ran over her hand, tepid, and strangely oily. She waited for it to become cooler, but it never did. She had to force herself to gulp down lukewarm sips, which made her feel even queasier.

On the wall panel, she read the temperature had flown up to forty-nine degrees Celsius, an unprecedented event. A brand-new record. There had been many casualties. There were, no doubt, going to be even more. Clarissa staggered back to the living room with difficulty. Her body felt stiff and heavy. She glanced outside, to the building facing hers. Hardly any lights on. The city seemed fast sleep. But shrill ambulance sirens and the drones' incessant circling came to her from afar. She felt sweaty. Her clothes were sticky. Was there a problem with the air-conditioning? She asked Mrs. Dalloway to check.

Two words lit up the panel.

SYSTEM ERROR.

Clarissa opened the front door. It was boiling on the landing, as if a heater had been turned on full blast. She went to fetch her mobile. Get hold of Jordan, Adelka. The calls couldn't go through, even though the signal was strong. She tried a dozen times, in vain. She remembered the landline in her office and rushed to it. When she stuck the phone to her ear, there was no dial tone, just an automatic voice blaring out the same words over and over: "System error. Please hang up. System error. Please hang up."

She was alone in her flat, with no air-conditioning, no mineral water. Up on the eighth floor, under a skylight that had warmed up all day long under the broiling sun. Perspiration trickled down the back of her neck, between her breasts. Dusk had barely been able to lower the heat. Her heart beat with slow, painful thumps. She could hear her blood flow through her eardrums with a muffled sucking noise that nauseated her. Her body had been drained of all the vigor she had left. She was a wreck. She couldn't move. It seemed to her the residence had depleted her of all her sap. She was nothing but an empty shell.

As she lay on the sofa, limp, inert, craving water, she felt she suddenly knew what "they" wanted, what "they" were doing. It was clear. How had she not seen it? She had to write it down, straight away. The floor swayed when she tried to get up. Above her head, the ceiling looked like waves were lapping over it. Hands stretched out in front of her, she ambled ahead warily. The screens on the walls weren't functioning properly; frames were skipping, appeared to be jumbled together, along with a crackling sound. New words popped up: *PROTOCOL C.A.S.A. DOWN. REBOOT.* Clarissa couldn't help smiling, in spite of her weariness. She imagined Dr. Dewinter and her team dripping with sweat, working themselves into a frenzy in front of their inoperative screens and servers. Somehow or other, the heat wave must have triggered the internal system's meltdown.

Clarissa got hold of her notebooks, tucked away in her handbag. She sat down to write, and had to put her pen down after a few sentences, she felt so weak. She shouldn't take all this lightly, at her age. She had to dampen her body, drink plenty of fluids. She had to act fast. Under the shower, she'd go. She'd wait it out there.

Impossible to stand up again. Her limbs had gone as flaccid as marshmallow candy. Flat on her stomach, she slid across the flooring, making feeble swimming movements. The remaining distance to the bathroom seemed never-ending. Sometimes she'd halt, spent. She felt like crying but forced herself not to. She certainly wasn't going to perish right there on her own floor! How pathetic! How ridiculous! She could hear her father's voice, his cursing, his wit. *Bloody hell! Move on, now! Come on, girl! Rustle your bustle!* Her elbows stung as she inched along. Each effort she made forced a strangled moan from her. The shower was miles away. She could very well stay right there, flat out, wheezing, drenched with perspiration, and no one would ever know. Cameras were no longer filming. She would peter out, just like that. In a few days, her body would be found by Ben, or by the nice cleaning lady who came once a week. Jordan and Andy would turn up beforehand; she was sure of that. At least she hoped so. It was tempting to let herself drop off. So very easy. The surface under her cheek felt hot and sticky.

As she stared close-up at the grooves engrained within the wooden planks, shadows began to materialize, created by the many indentations; tormented features appeared, sketched here and there as if by magic: malevolent eyes, grimacing mouths, crooked noses. It seemed to her the floorboards were covered with a chain of scowling masks, hideous hobgoblins with emaciated faces like in Munch's powerful painting, *The Scream*. She forced her eyes away, but when she glanced at the walls, she noticed with anguish blurry shapes coming to life there as well, as if the corridor were crowded with apparitions hiding behind partitions, reaching out to grab her.

Clarissa shut her eyes. That was better. They had gone. She breathed slowly, using Elise's method. Should she surrender to this gentle stupor? Should she let herself be carried away? *Are you off your rocker, girl? Blast it, that's enough!* Her father's voice, calling her by that first name she hated.

She raised her head, gritted her teeth with all the forcefulness she could muster. *Keep moving. Keep going forward. Inch by inch.* The goblins had vanished. She had to reach the shower. A trembling frame caught her eye—a square image appearing on the luminous panel at the end of the passageway. Clarissa made slow progress, puffing and panting. The palms of her hands were sore; she had cramps in her legs. She was able to make out a sort of index card with an ID photo. She drew closer, managed to heave herself to her knees with a final effort. She didn't have her glasses on, and she stuck her nose to the screen.

SURNAME: PERRIER
FIRST NAME: JIM
AGE: 35

She couldn't figure out what it was, why she was seeing this. Jim's card faded away, then popped back up on the unit.

CONSTITUTIONAL SIGNS: ALCOHOLIC. DRUG ADDICT. PARANOID PERSONALITY DISORDER.

The display went black. She squealed with frustration. Then other cards emerged, too fast for her to see them properly. The heat must have affected the servers. Everything C.A.S.A. knew and was hiding had somehow become visible. Were all the artists of the residence witnessing this confidential data right now? Or was this only happening in her place? The frames shuffled by in a quick frenzy.

At times, the system switched off, then lit up again. Suddenly, she thought she saw her own index card, only for a split second, her features looking bonier than ever, and a long paragraph, where a chunk of words reached out to slap her: *PRONE TO DEPRESSION.*

Her anger outdid her weakness, and she shot to her feet with new vigor, her entire body quaking with resentment. She wasn't going to give in to this. Never. She was going to flee. She had to prove all this. She had to photograph those index cards, keep it all as evidence. She turned back to get her mobile. Another dizzy spell slowed her down. She was forced to stop and lean against the wall, catching her breath. Her skin felt clammy. There was no air.

When she came back with her phone, the panel had gone dark once more. She hung around. It did not light up again. Had she imagined it all? After fifteen minutes, she went to the shower, weary and uneasy. She couldn't make out the difference between the hobgoblins on the floorboards and the index cards. What had she truly perceived? Had it all been in her mind? She undressed, taking her time, feeling the shakiness take over her body again. The mirror sent back a ghostly echo. Who was watching her, back there? Who could see her? She held up her middle finger wordlessly, with a bitter smirk. Once she got under the shower, tap open, she huddled there, back against the wall. The water was still lukewarm. She shut her eyes, let the stream flow into her mouth, her ears. The trickle of the running water had a calming effect. She thought back to what she had read about Jim Perrier. Alcohol. Drugs. Paranoia. What should she make of it?

Something moving startled her. It was the cat. He stared at her thoughtfully, sitting across from her.

"Hop on in, old sport. It'll do you good."

She had always heard cats hated water, but against all expectation, Chablis let out a small mew and leaped over to land by her side. He let himself get entirely wet, then, with his customary daintiness, installed himself on her thighs and began to purr.

She was still asleep when the doorbell rang. She had no idea of the time; she only remembered having closed the tap, flung herself onto her bed, wrapped in a humid towel. The room temperature seemed agreeably cool. She slipped into a bathrobe and checked the control panel. It was Ben, more good-humored than usual, with an embarrassed expression.

"Everything okay, Mrs. Katsef?"

"Not really. I only just woke up."

He explained the system had undergone a gigantic breakdown and that the air-conditioning had stopped functioning. But it had all been fixed.

"I see," she said. "I nearly kicked the bucket."

He gazed at her, confused.

"Oh, my gosh!"

"I guess I'm tougher than I look. What about the other artists?"

"Most of them left the residence before it got too hot. Have you seen the news?"

"No."

"Everything collapsed, all over the city. Breakdown, failure, outage. No signal, no surveillance, hacked databases, burglaries. Melted asphalt. And lots of casualties."

"Indeed . . . Do you need anything?"

"Yes, Dr. Dewinter would like all artists who went through the heat wave to pass a medical test. I need to check everything's working properly."

Then he added, "You look very pale, if you don't mind my saying so."

She did not answer, only glared back at him. While he was in the bathroom, she checked her phone. It was just past nine. Numerous calls and texts. She went to the kitchen, opened the refrigerator. Staring at her in the face were four bottles of mineral water. The ones she had looked for in vain last night. She sighed.

She went back to reading her texts. Jordan was fraught, so

were Andy, Toby, François, and a couple of other friends. How was she? Could she respond? Was everything okay? She tried to answer them fast, Jordan first. Yes, it had been dreadful, the air-conditioning broke down, everything else broke down, she had never been so thirsty, hot, and faint in her life, but she was okay! Jordan texted back, relieved. She'd call later on today.

As Clarissa was getting back to Andy, her phone rang. It was Laure-Marie, her publisher. She picked up immediately. Laure-Marie wanted to know if she'd survived. Laughingly, Clarissa said that she had, but when she thought of the acute nausea, the vanishing mineral water, the goblins appearing on the floorboards, she wondered if she hadn't underestimated what she had gone through. Laure-Marie wanted to get back in touch. They hadn't seen each other for a while. Apparently, Clarissa had moved. What about getting together for a drink? That way, Clarissa could tell her about her new project, because Laure-Marie was waiting to hear about it! Clarissa agreed to call her later on that week.

Her project. Her book. At a standstill. By eroding her energy, devastating her sleep, filming her around-the-clock, C.A.S.A. had crushed her desire to write. All this was part of their plan, which she understood last night. She'd have to get hold of Andy, too, to tell her what she had discovered. Clarissa already knew she was not going to call her publisher. She hadn't made enough progress. She had to get out of here first. She had to find out how. The lyrics of Toby's favorite song, "Hotel California," kept coming back to her: She could check out anytime she wanted, but she could never leave.

Ben was still in the bathroom, fiddling. He must have sensed her impatience, because he came out looking self-conscious. He informed her everything was in order. The test would take a while longer, he said. But she had to go through with it. Dr. Dewinter had insisted all artists should.

"Fine," said Clarissa grimly. "I just can't wait."

He gawked at her again, lost.

"Good-bye, Ben," she said icily.

He scurried out. Clarissa headed into the bathroom and faced the mirror, looking into the two small red specks.

"Hello, Clarissa," said a mechanical male voice. "Please place your palm on the inlay."

Clarissa obeyed. She couldn't help noticing how gaunt she looked. She had lost weight, which was confirmed when she stepped on the scales.

"Please answer the following questions, Clarissa. Did you faint during the heat wave?"

"No," she replied.

"Did you feel dizzy and lose your balance?"

"Yes."

"Did you feel thirsty?"

"Yes."

"Did your urine appear darker?"

"I didn't pay attention."

"Did you have any cramps?"

"Yes, in my legs."

"Did you have any hallucinations?"

"No."

"Please put your hand back on the inlay."

She noticed the voice had switched from French to English. She put her hand back.

The voice repeated, "Did you have any hallucinations during the heat wave?"

There was no way she was going to admit she'd seen imps in the patterns of the wooden floor.

"No."

"Did you feel weak?"

"Yes."

"Did your head ache?"

"Yes."

"Were you nauseous?"

"Yes."

"There are eyeglasses on your left. Please put them on. Face the mirror and place your palm on the inlay."

Ben had left glasses near the sink. She positioned them on her nose. They blurred her vision slightly. A dull whine started in her left ear.

"Please keep your eyes open, Clarissa."

The whine became more powerful, like a mighty hum, digging deep into her head. She felt the noise spiraling into her brain like a drill.

"What is this?" she muttered.

"Please refrain from talking. Do not remove your hand. Please look at the marks in the mirror."

How long was she going to remain docile? Was she really going to stand there, let them get on with this? What were they doing? Trying to read what she was thinking? Pilfering her brain?

The voice had gone back to French. She hardly noticed. She tried to stand straight, but the intensifying hum made her shudder and feel giddy.

"Please remain still."

She felt convinced she knew what was going on. She had read about those scientists probing the brain's electrical activity, trying to read into inner thoughts.

"Look into the mirror, please. Describe what you see."

She saw her own face, as long and thin as Virginia Woolf's. With eyes as blue as Romain Gary's.

"I see myself."

"What else do you see, please?"

She noticed an image had been projected within the glass. It looked like a revolving sphere.

"I see a circle."

"Describe it, please."

"In French or in English?"

A pause.

"They" hadn't expected that, she thought, gloating.

"Don't choose a language consciously. Just describe what you see, please."

She described the glittery circle, using French and English at the same time, flawlessly switching from one to the other. Speaking very fast, still using both languages, she invented elements she did not see at all—a tree, a lake, a house. She went into detail. It was almost fun.

"Please describe what you see."

"That's what I'm doing."

"There is no house, lake, or tree in the mirror."

"Really? Well, I see them. You don't?"

The humming noise was strong now, nearly unbearable. What the hell was in those glasses? Electrodes? Captors? What were "they" up to, exactly? Delving into her neurons, certainly. Resistance began to take shape within her, and she gave full force to that defiance. She watched her inner retaliation thrive; it was like a blue glow hurling itself against the humming noise, casting a screen all around, engulfing Clarissa, making the mirror and the space around her disappear. The hum could no longer get through the blue, no matter how hard it tried. *Don't give them what they want. Don't let them see what's inside your head. Keep all those thoughts to yourself. They can't take thoughts from you if you don't let them.* Clarissa forced her eyes to remain open, visualizing the blue glow becoming stronger, thicker, and deeper, fighting the powerful grinding whine with every cell in her body, every pulsation of her heart. It was like a merciless battle against the demented storm raging inside her mind.

"Please relax," said the voice.

The blue radiance became her language, neither French nor

English; it became her own language, expressing complete pugnacity, and that words were no longer needed in order to clarify she was not going to let "them" into her mind. How long did the combat last? She had no idea. The whining finally decreased. She was asked to take the glasses off. She felt drained.

"Thank you, Clarissa. Medical examination completed."

She tottered into the toilet, bolted the door; it was the only spot in the flat that remained an intimate space. She grinned at the irony of it. She slid down, back to the wall, tried to rest. To her consternation, she sensed the intense weakness she'd felt last night creep its way back into her organism. She must gain her strength back. She had to make plans. She had to act fast.

Clarissa rubbed her hands over her face, trying to give herself some energy. She breathed slowly in and out. She didn't care if no one believed her. Maybe only Andy would. It didn't matter. She knew what to do next.

Nathalie's bookstore-café, on boulevard du Montparnasse, was packed this morning, despite the tragic events of yesterday. Customers gathered around displays, settled into cozy armchairs, or sat down for coffee and cake. Clarissa hadn't been back since the opening. She was cheered to see so many bookworms on the premises. A young salesperson informed her that Nathalie was upstairs, in her office. She'd go fetch her. Clarissa wandered through the stalls. She realized she hadn't done much reading since her move. The residence had dispossessed her of her love of books. No writing, no reading. What a punishment.

"My God, Clarissa!"

Nathalie had gasped with shock.

"You're so thin!"

"I know. I didn't do it on purpose, believe me. And the heat didn't help, either. But don't worry, I'm fine."

She flashed a large smile to reassure her friend. But Nathalie wasn't fooled by it. Clarissa changed the subject, asking her about her shop. Nathalie answered with her usual fervor, going into the details of the highs and lows of bookselling. Clarissa listened with pleasure. Then she said, "I was wondering if I could ask you a small favor."

"Of course! What is it?"

"Your friend, the one I met here, who works in real estate."

"Guillaume? I heard he helped you find your new flat."

"That's him. Could you call him for me?"

"You want his number?"

"I already have his number. But I'd rather not call him from my mobile."

"Oh?"

"Could you possibly call him on your own phone? And then put me on?"

Nathalie looked at her closely. Clarissa knew what she was thinking, right there. That Clarissa looked like a demented old lady, with her red dye going to pot and her intense blue gaze.

"You need to talk to him?"

"Yes."

"A problem with your flat?"

"Sort of. I simply need to ask him one quick question. It won't take very long."

Slight hesitation.

"Okay. All right."

Nathalie fished her phone from her pocket. She pressed on a key, waited, and got voice mail.

"Hi, Guillaume. It's Nat. Can you get back to me? Important. Thanks."

Clarissa said she'd wait around, looking at books. She wouldn't be far. Nathalie got on with her work. Clarissa's eyes followed her as she gave advice to clients, located books for them. She never seemed to lose her zeal. Clarissa remembered most of her own books were still with François. She still had many belongings in her old place. One day, she'd have to retrieve them. But not while she was at the residence. François's letter was at the bottom of her bag, with her notebooks. She still hadn't read it. She held it between her fingertips. It felt quite thick.

Just as she was thinking of opening it, Nathalie was back, flourishing her mobile.

"Here's Guillaume."

Clarissa took the phone.

"Hello," she said in what she hoped was a jovial voice. "I'm not sure you remember me? We met here, at Nathalie's opening."

"The red-haired author who writes about houses and suicidal authors, not easily forgotten," he replied with a slightly sarcastic intonation. "What can I do for you?"

Nathalie had gone back to her customers. Clarissa was alone.

"I wanted to talk to you about the C.A.S.A. residence."

"I believe you live there, right? So you got in! Well done! That's no easy feat, and they're rather picky, I hear."

She nearly added "And I'm longing to get out of it," but abstained.

"That's right, I was admitted. Sorry for putting this to you so bluntly, but what is C.A.S.A., exactly? Who is behind it?"

He seemed surprised.

"Well, benefactors keen on promoting all forms of artistic creations. They have huge financial resources."

"Have you met anyone from C.A.S.A.?"

"I must have crossed paths with a couple of people, but I don't remember. I only know Clémence Dutilleul, whom I put you in touch with. She's in charge of finding artists for the residence. That's all I know. I worked with my architects to construct the place. I don't know much more about C.A.S.A."

"Nothing at all?"

"No! What are you getting at? What's with these people?"

"You weren't aware, for instance, that all the artists living in the residence are filmed?"

A pause.

"Filmed all the time?" he asked.

"Yes. All the time. We signed a contract."

"So you agreed to it?"

"That's not the issue. I want to find out *why* we are filmed."

"Surveillance requirements, no doubt. Aren't you happy up there on the eighth floor? Your studio is magnificent! The number of people who'd love to be in your shoes!"

"Have you met Dr. Dewinter?"

"No, I haven't. Who is this person?"

"An artificial intelligence specialist. She runs the C.A.S.A. protocol."

"So?"

"You don't see the link?"

"I'm afraid not."

"You don't see how an AI expert could find a household of artists most interesting?"

"I'm sorry, ma'am, I fail to see the link, and don't see how I can help you in any way."

Clarissa was unable to keep him on the phone. He asked to be handed back to Nathalie. She heard his voice boom out to her friend: "What a dotty old lady!"

Clarissa took off, thanking Nathalie, who kept watching her with a mixture of suspicion and concern. She walked along the boulevard, noting how yesterday's temperatures had left traces in the extenuated features of passersby, in their slow shuffle. Clarissa hadn't listened to the news, or read the press on her tablet. Fatalities, bedlam, confusion, crisis, pessimism. The same old song. She'd answered each text message she received, including François's. She had written, *All OK, and you?* He'd replied, *Yes, thanks. Did you get my letter?* She'd left it at that.

For the moment, C.A.S.A. was her prime concern. What they wanted, how they got what they wanted, and, above all, how to leave them. She had always known how to weave intimate connections with homes. The place she'd shared with Toby, on rue d'Alésia, left sweet memories in her mind, in spite of the tragedy that had befallen them. It was a bright, cheerful two-room flat. She could still see Toby sitting on the little balcony, reading in the sunlight. She had also been fond of the larger apartment, acquired with François, on rue Henri-Barbusse, the one she'd decorated with him, full of her beloved books. She had loved writing there.

Like foreign territory barring her entry, her apartment in the residence spread out in front of her, and she perceived hostility in every nook, every chink. Perhaps she was not wanted here because she refused to cooperate. She gave nothing away; she did not submit. Were the other artists easier to manage and to influence? Were they content merely living and working here, having no inkling concerning the truth? Was she the only one seeing that truth? Jim Perrier had come close. Had he been dismissed because of his misgivings? Or because of his addictions, which didn't conform to the C.A.S.A. protocol? And what about her? Did she risk being expelled, as well? Her insubordination had not gone unnoticed. Dr. Dewinter herself had turned up to call her to order. Perhaps that was the way out. Disobedience. Well, she was ready. She was more than ready.

Back in the bathroom, she avoided looking at herself in the mirror. She made sure each of her gestures seemed calm and ordinary. She acted the same way in the kitchen. An internal message from Adelka showed up on the screens. She was wondering how Clarissa'd put up with the awful heat. She herself had gone off to a friend's place, near Lille. Clarissa dictated a concise reply: *Yes, thanks, all fine, but it was dreadful! See you soon!* Her mobile buzzed as she was cleaning things up in the kitchen.

It was her brother, Arthur. She hadn't spoken to him directly

since the choppy outcome of Aunt Serena's will. She'd sent an
email thanking him for the brooch, without alluding to its real
worth. Even if she didn't feel like hearing the sound of his voice,
she took the call. Arthur sounded out of breath. It was about their
father. A rapid fright shot through her. Their dad had had a bad
fall; he'd broken two ribs and his nose. He was in the hospital.
Could she come? He was also going to alert Jordan.

Of course she'd go. But how was their dad? What happened?
Arthur said he hadn't yet spoken to the doctors. Their father fell
out of his bed. Luckily, the nursing assistant who was on duty was
able to help. He was at the brand-new London Fields hospital,
near Broadway Market.

Clarissa remembered the ticket she'd recently booked for her
upcoming London trip. She was able to modify it for a new one;
the train was departing in two hours. She stuffed a change of
clothes and toiletries into a travel bag. She had no idea how long
she might have to stay. The cat! What was she going to do with
it? Adelka seemed to be the only solution. With Chablis tucked
under her arm, she went down to the fourth floor. Wearing a
jumpsuit, with a paintbrush in hand, Adelka opened up.

"My dad's in the hospital, in London. I've got to leave."

"Oh, your poor dad! You want me to keep this precious bundle?
I'll take care of the food and the litter, don't you worry!"

Clarissa thanked her warmly. She had to make her way in time
to the sprawling Gare du Nord, a place she disliked all the more
because of its never-ending overhaul. Her British passport enabled
her to skip endless queues at control checks, but there was still
customs to go through, on either end. It had been getting worse
and worse, ever since Brexit's unsettling consequences, steeped in
complication. One had still to wait for hours in order to set foot on
the island where she was born. How strange it was to originate from
these two neighboring countries, traditional foes, which, over time,
had not succeeded in becoming closer, but, on the contrary, had

drawn even further apart. Like most people she knew, Clarissa found Eurostar's new name, StarExpress, ridiculous.

She tried to get hold of Jordan but only got through to voice mail. She wondered if her daughter had managed to make herself available, and if she was en route to London. During the entire trip, her father stayed on her mind. Arthur sent her the hospital room number. At St. Pancras, during the second interminable wait at customs, she did her best to remain patient. No use getting edgy. She had to save all her energy up for her father. She took the Tube to Hackney. She was usually elated to be back in her native city, but today, the joy had gone. It felt sad admitting it, but all those years spent in Paris had turned her into a Frenchwoman. London was no longer her home. Her French side had taken over. Was this irreversible? she wondered. Perhaps it was fleeting, due to fragility and fatigue.

Leaving the Tube station at Bethnal Green, she walked briskly to the nearby hospital. Her legs were painful, her joints stiff. She couldn't help daydreaming about the summer holidays Jordan was planning with the brooch money. Puglia, in southern Italy, was the chosen destination. Jordan had discovered a *masseria,* a fortified farmhouse, lost within a field of thousand-year-old olive trees, miraculously preserved from the disease that had eradicated most of them. The deep blue sea was only a few kilometers away.

The shiny modern façade drew itself up in front of her. Clarissa paused for a few seconds before entering. The state her father might be in worried her. He was so old, so vulnerable.

Arthur was waiting for her outside the room, with his daughters. He seemed glum.

"Brace yourself," he said, hugging her. Clarissa greeted her sniffling nieces.

She stepped into the room alone, not feeling very reassured. Her father's face was bruised, entirely black-and-blue. A huge bump deformed his forehead; a bandage covered his nose, and an intravenous drip was fitted in his arm. He was unrecognizable.

She couldn't refrain from bursting into tears. Her exhaustion overcame her in one powerful wave. She could only stand there, weeping, feeling as helpless as a child. Her dad! Her old beloved dad! She couldn't bear seeing him this way.

"My darling! My sweetie!"

Her father's unmistakable voice piped up, weak but still full of humor. Dumbfounded, she opened her eyes.

"Honey, why are you in such a state? It's only a blasted tumble! Can you imagine, falling from your own bed? Bloody hell! Arthur's got a face like a month of wet Sundays! And his daughters, just as bad, a couple of twits!"

Clarissa couldn't help laughing through her tears. She couldn't get over it. He was incredible! Sitting next to the bed, she clenched her father's long, wrinkled hand. She admitted her apprehension, and how his devastated features had shocked her.

Her father chortled.

"Well, my hour has not yet come. I'm all bashed up, but I'm still here! And I'm so happy to see you. Come closer so I can look at your pretty face. Oh! You're looking under the weather! What's with those little eyes? You've lost weight, my dearest. You've got me fretted now."

A topsy-turvy world! Her injured father, worrying about her.

"I'm okay, Dad. Don't worry. How long are you here for?"

"Speak a little louder, my love; the chip in my ear is kicking up."

Clarissa repeated her question.

"No idea! In this damned hospital, robots look after patients. Robots never make mistakes with their diagnosis, do they? They're the kings of the world, right? What's left for us poor humans?"

"Emotions?" quipped Clarissa.

"Spot-on. But what about you, my sweet? How's your book coming along? Are you happy with it?"

"No. I'm not happy, Dad. I can't work properly in my apartment."

"Now, that's the last straw!" said her father. "You and houses! Ever since you were small, they've had a hold on you. So what's wrong with the flat?"

Clarissa prepared herself to reveal the entire C.A.S.A. inside story to him, to go into detail, to see how he would react. She was looking forward to sharing with her father what she was going through.

The door slid open and she saw Jordan standing on the threshold. Her daughter moaned when she discovered her grandfather's discolored face. Then Arthur rushed in as well, with his daughters. Her father was surrounded by his loving family. In spite of his contusions, he glowed with happiness. He was thrilled to have them all there; it was Christmas in June! Only Andy was missing. A nurse barged in to tell them they were making too much noise. And a maximum of two people could remain at the bedside.

Clarissa ended up with her daughter and her father. They all decided to favor those who had come from afar. And those who'd endured those endless lines to get into this bloody country, grumbled Jordan, while her father roared with laughter. Clarissa noticed (how could she not notice?) that Jordan had installed an infinitesimal distance between them. Jordan glanced at her, smiled, but the detachment was well and truly there, growing by the minute, and she felt upset. She'd very rarely perceived a cold shoulder coming from her daughter. She could not understand what was going on. In her mind, she went back to all the conversations she'd recently had with her. She couldn't pick out anything in particular. What about Andy? Her instinct told her that must be it. Perhaps Jordan was cross with Clarissa because of Andy. She could hardly believe it. Was Jordan irritated because of the closeness she and Andy shared? Clarissa was aware Andy was most probably difficult with her mother, like any teenager. She knew she shared an exceptional relationship with her granddaughter.

The nurse interrupted them to say it was time to tend to the patient. They were asked to leave the room. Clarissa said good-bye to